Their Chosen Home

D1545602

Richard Brian Clark

outskirts
press

Outskirts Press, Inc.
http://www.outskirtspress.com

ISBN: 978-1-9772-3509-1

PRINTED IN THE UNITED STATES OF AMERICA

Dedication

Their Chosen Home is dedicated to my father and mother, John and Margaret (Cook) Clark. My father was born in the early 1900's in Preston, England an industrial mill-town. In the 1920's, my grandfather and my dad immigrated to the United States and settled in Pawtucket, Rhode Island. They worked in textile mills in order to raise money to bring the rest of their family to America. By 1925 my grandmother and two aunts crossed the ocean and joined the rest of the family in Pawtucket.

My mother's family immigrated to the United States from Blackburn, England as a family unit in 1926. They also made their home in the Pawtucket area. My mother and father did not meet until they both attended the same church and sang in the choir. They each loved this country while truly expressing a passion for America and its history which they passed on to me. They embraced their new home by becoming Naturalized American Citizens. "Their Chosen Home" eventually became Kenyon Avenue, Pawtucket, Rhode Island, USA. It was also my home until I joined the USAF in 1960.

Introduction

Writing this novel brought back interesting memories in my life while causing me to realize just how some things never seem to change. Segregation in this country still exists in many ways. It seems our politicians can't help but play the race card whenever confronted with a legitimate argument or situation they just refuse to deal with. Back in 1960 I entered the United States Air Force, and was soon stationed at Lackland Air Force Base in San Antonio Texas. Coming from Rhode Island, I'd had zero contact with black people. Being in the South was really a wakeup call for me. My closest friend on base was a Black airman from Washington, DC. We were both seventeen years of age. On our first day spent downtown San Antonio together, I was totally blindsided seeing "Whites Only" signs posted in windows. Walking into a restaurant an employee confronted us looking directly at me while saying, "We don't serve colored here." I eventually had an apartment off base that was owned by the nicest elderly couple you could ever want to know. But they were Southern born and raised and were strict Roosevelt

Democrats. They did not want a black person on their property under any circumstance and made this perfectly clear to me the first time my Air Force friend visited me.

Eventually the Air Force saw fit to assign me to a medical unit just south of Verdun in France. I found Europe to be truly color blind. During my time assigned in France, I managed to visit Germany, Austria, Belgium, England and Luxemburg. Never once in these travels did I encounter problems related to race. Returning to America, I finished out my four year tour of duty at Otis Air Force Base in Massachusetts. John F Kennedy was now President, and the civil rights issue was in total crisis. Martin Luther King was in Washington telling Americans that he had a dream. George Wallace, the Governor of Alabama, was standing on the Alabama State Capital steps saying "Segregation now and Segregation forever." Young people from Massachusetts were riding busses down south to protest segregation.

Writing this story, I tried to envision what it would have been like following the Civil War for my main characters traveling out west together. I also came to realize the monumental changes that had taken place in such a short period of time. When they began their journey, a tragic civil war had just recently ended. Wagons were rolling westward across this great country, while many of the people from those wagons were actually walking westward. Coming right behind them was the railroad, what the Native American's called "The Iron Horse." Soon thereafter the airplane would follow. All this change coming within one person's lifetime. A young Simon could have experienced it all.

I tried to imagine my character's thoughts as they looked

at an expansive grassy plain before them covered seemingly to the horizon with a large herd of Buffalo. Or when they first saw a trolley running on rails down 4th or 10th street in St. Louis. Beginning their journey west, there was no such thing as triple A. No roadmaps. No Howard Johnsons or Holiday Inn's. Often only word of mouth would advise them of what possibly lay ahead as they moved ever so slowly forward day after day. And at the start of their journey, they were truly alone. It was a lawless time, and so they went armed. A small, maybe six or eight foot open wagon held all their possessions. There were no shocks on their wagon. Leather straps cushioned their rough ride as best they could. Canvas alone protected them and the contents of their wagon from the elements.

US Soldiers, both black and white, guarded small sections of our country in wooden forts often scattered far and wide across our great land. Native Americans: Sioux, Cheyenne, Pawnee, Blackfoot and Crow along with many other indigenous tribes watched as whites invaded their land, eventually claiming total possession. We Americans termed it our "Manifest Destiny."

I can only imagine their feelings of apprehension at the very first sight of the mountains that appeared to block their way forward. To be alone in what was considered at the time to be the middle of nowhere, understandably would make one welcome the companionship of a wagon train. But think of that Black Bear breaking branches just yards away from your wagon, and this was still only Pennsylvania. That hoped-for wagon train was waiting, but in truth it was still almost a thousand miles west of you. Yet to come would be the complete terror brought on by the howls just outside their wagon, as wolves sniffed at the night air laden with the smell of wood smoke and food being cooked. Yes, our westward movement was indeed an adventure unlike anything before, or anything that would come later. Today through parts of our land, one can still see, and actually reach down and touch, the ruts in the Earth caused by the many wagon wheels that rolled westward over the Oregon and Santa Fe trails well over a hundred years ago.

With possibly only the music of a violin or guitar, our pioneers danced beside a wood fire on a black night, not knowing what the morning would bring. Far from being a Wal-Mart, a simple small Sutter shop at a fort held the promise of new shoes, or possibly even the opportunity to write and send a letter back east. Some people looked at the mountains before them and decided to turn back. Wagons were traded or upgraded, with Conestoga wagons being the wagons of choice for the long trek through the difficult, often mountainous, country that lay ahead.

Often it was at an Army post that people going west first encountered Native Americans. For the most part, these were friendly Indians. Settlers were awed by the functional Teepee, and even the clothes worn by these people. Porcupine quills, and colored beads adorned much of the Native's clothing. Cloth was seldom seen. Animal skins and tanned hides made up most of their clothing. Moccasins were the choice for footwear among all the Natives. They actually scoffed at the thick black leather shoes our pioneers wore.

Sometime around 1950, my Mother and Father took me from Rhode Island, out to California to visit with Uncles,

Aunts and my cousins. I remember riding in the Southern Pacific's large red and yellow train, with its gleaming aluminum observation carriages, from Chicago to Los Angeles California. I know my nose was pressed against the glass, looking to see Cowboys and Indians. This was, after all, the hay day of the Hollywood Westerns. But the truth be known, all I saw was endless open spaces. Los Angeles was also far bigger than our State Capital back at Providence, Rhode Island. The only "flavor" of the old west I experienced while in Los Angeles, was when we visited Olvera St. This was what today we would refer to as a flea market. But it was Mexican through and through. I remember mostly the friendliness of the people there. I remember also Knott's Berry Farm in California with its buckboard wagons and false store fronts. I believed movie director John Ford's take on the west was far better.

But this story of Simon and Darlene held a special interest for me as I put words to paper. In many instances as in my past novels, it presented a culture clash. A clash between Native Americans and westward moving pioneers. A culture clash between blacks and whites. A culture clash that in a broader sense for some strange reason exists even today. Maybe today it is just a good time to return and reflect upon American Indians riding on painted ponies. Instead of attempting to re-write our history, we should revel in all that we have accomplished in our little over 200 years here.

Our history is so special, so unique. As a people we took on England, the greatest military empire at the time when we chose to rule ourselves and not be ruled by a King from across an ocean. Our founding fathers pledged their sacred honor, and gambled their very lives in the hope of producing a new nation where Americans would truly be free. Yes many of them owned slaves. It was a fact of the time, impossible to be judged fairly against values that exist among us over two hundred years later. It took almost one hundred years to end slavery in America. Approximately 600,000 American soldiers died in our Civil War along with countless civilians. But slavery was forever banished from our country. Never must we allow the basic good coming out of these conflicts to be forgotten. Rewriting history will leave us with no history at all. We cannot, and collectively must not, let this happen. History, it is what has happened, what has gone before. It must never be forgotten, denied or erased. History should always be treated as a learning opportunity.

Monuments throughout our country tell the story and history of our past. To even think, today, that there are those among us who are joyous at the toppling of a statue of George Washington, is to this writer, beyond belief. Yes, the father of our country owned slaves. But I can cite ten times throughout our Revolutionary War, when he saved this great country by seeing to it that America could become the country that people from around the world would desire to immigrate while hoping to seek freedom and a better life. And just so we never forget, George Washington freed his slaves before he died. I consider him a very special man and somewhat ahead of his time.

Let all Americans today think on Abraham Lincoln's second inaugural given just weeks before his assassination. Andrew Johnson, a war Democrat added to the ticket as

Vice President to bolster electoral support in border-states, arrived at the inauguration dead drunk.

Republican Abraham Lincoln then delivered the last great speech of his life. He invoked God. He mentioned the Bible. He promised to eradicate slavery. **"With malice toward none, with charity for all, with firmness in the right, as God gives us to see the right, let us strive to finish the work we are in, to bind up the nation's wounds, to care for him who shall have borne the battle, and for his widow and his orphan."**

Lincoln made a point of not differentiating between Northern and Southern veterans or between black and white soldiers within the Union Army. A little over two hundred years later, it would do us well to remember our past with honesty.

Chapter 1
The Journey Begins

"Beats me as to just why you, or anyone else here-about, should be interested in my doings, but I'll answer your questions and tell you the truth as best as I can recall." Simon said while sitting in a chair across from Jessie Smith, the reporter for the Lexington News.

"Well you were one of the first persons to settle here in Lexington and look where you are today. You're about to attend your first meeting as a member of the new Lexington Planning Board and who knows what that will lead to. I've heard people talking regarding you even being put up for Mayor. You own a gun store located on Main Street and represent Colt firearms. You've fought hostile Indians and according to what I've been told, you've killed and buried a few also. You've relocated to a new home you've built just outside of town. And most everyone has questions about the grave site on your property. I for one am telling you I've heard at least five different stories regarding that grave, and I do believe if nothing else it's time questions regarding that issue should be answered and put to rest once and for all." Jessie pushed back a lock of hair that had fallen crossing her face while she had been talking. "Maybe we can start right off with this Darlene person?" She asked.

"Now I'm sure you've noticed that I'm black," Simon said as a smile broke across his face. "So I'll be asking you to be patient with me. I'll be doing my best to tell you everything I can, but I'll have to be starting at what I consider is really the beginning of this story. And I'll be asking you right off to forgive me if I don't mince words. I figure to tell it like it is, and people can think what they will.

"Now my having been a slave, I never learned my letters as you have. In my time this was just not allowed, actually I suspect it was against the law. I can tell you as sure as I'm sitting here, that I saw both black men and women who had whips taken to their backs until their blood ran freely in a dozen or more places because they'd been caught trying to learn to read.

"I could start this story at Pemberton since this was the plantation I was taken to shortly after being sold at the auction building in Savannah where I arrived following my capture in Africa. And before I forget, let me set things straight right off about my being a slave. I was captured by my own kind. Blacks in Africa took and sold me into slavery. Now I saw some whites on the ship that brought me over to this country, but most every other slave I've come across tells me the same story.

"So I'm going to begin by telling you about Darlene. Now I don't believe you'll understand much of anything I'll be telling you about Darlene being as young as you are. But believe me, I'm not going to water-down anything I'll be saying regarding her and me." Simon paused and appeared to be deep in thought. One or two minutes passed before he smiled and began speaking once again.

"OK, I'll start by telling you I was at Pemberton Plantation a little over two, maybe three years, near as I can remember, when I first came face to face and actually had words with Darlene. She was the plantation owner's wife, and trust me when I say that she was one right good looking lady. Now if anyone had ever told me that her and I would spend almost ten years, and cross a good portion of this country together, why I'd have laughed right in their face. I'm thinking I was about nineteen, maybe twenty, that first time she and I ever spoke to each other.

"She caught me swimming when I was supposed to be out working in the field. I was as naked as a Jay bird when she ordered me out of the water. Lucky for me, I was doing a task for Blue at the time. Now Blue was the head black on this plantation, and I have to believe since I was actually doing something for him, this saved my young ass.

"Blue was about the best man I'd ever met since I was brought across the ocean from my home in Africa. I can't say as I ever knew his real name. Blue stood a full six feet tall, and Pemberton was the second plantation he'd landed at. At his first plantation they made indigo and his hands along with half way up his arms were as blue as blue could be. That's how he got his name and somehow it stuck. Blue was a gentle person, always spoke softly, but when he spoke people listened. Now his hair wasn't kinky like most blacks. He kept it short and I'd guess fifty times a day he ran a comb that he'd made, through it.

"He didn't talk with an African accent like the other slaves on the plantation. That first year I knew him he'd slip into his African accent now and then, but he always caught himself. When that happened he'd stop dead in whatever he was saying, turn and walk three or four feet away, pause for a minute or so and then turn and come back and begin speaking again. It was like he'd wiped away what he'd said the first time and now he'd speak slowly making sure that not a hint of African showed in his speech.

"Blue took a liking to me right off and I felt the same about him. When I got myself in real danger over my being close to the plantation owner's wife, It was Blue that covered for me, and it was Blue that finally told me I had to get away from Pemberton. He could just as easily have turned me over to Mr. James Temper, the overseer of Pemberton Plantation, or to Darlene's husband. I've little or no doubt it would have been a hanging tree for me for sure had that been the case.

"Good Lord but Darlene was one of a kind. I'm telling you that I've looked at and crossed a good part of the Atlantic Ocean, stood in the Bahamas along with being most everywhere up north, and as God is my judge I can look you or anyone else right in the eye and say I wouldn't wish to ever forget so much as even one of those years I spent with that woman.

"Well, back at Pemberton Planation Darlene took me to her bed while her husband who was the owner of the plantation was off at Richmond, Virginia representing South Carolina. I'd spent some loving time with her on and off the plantation when it became obvious to many what was going on between her and I. Blue finally took me aside and told me it had been voted among our people that I had to get away from Pemberton. Now Blue could have just arranged with the overseer James Temper to have me exchanged for someone at another plantation. But he and I both knew that would have solved nothing.

"Only God knows how I hated having to leave my friends at Pemberton, especially Blue. He'd been a friend to me since I'd first arrived at Pemberton. Anyhow, that very night I went into the woods off the north end of the plantation and didn't stop running until it was light enough for me to see about fifty yards ahead of where I stood. Now you got to be understanding there was a Civil War raging, and blacks were constantly running away from plantations all throughout the South. Hawkers were scouring the woods capturing any slave they could find that was on the run. Once caught, a run-away became a ten-dollar gold piece or even more to a Hawker once returned to the plantation he'd run from.

"Well that first morning as I stood stock still looking ahead trying to see everything up ahead of me that might smack of danger, I also took stock of myself and realized I was what you'd call a sorry sight to say the least. During that first night I'd run through the woods as if the Devil himself was after me. Branches, briers and thorns tore at my clothing, and I can't remember from how many places I was bleeding. Nothing serious really, scratches mainly. Months later I thought back upon that night and realized how foolish I'd been. Jonathan Pemberton was at Richmond the night I ran away from the plantation, so the foreman would not have posted me as a run-away until the owner returned and he'd have had a chance to explain the situation regarding my running away. Therefore, there would also be no hounds set loose tracking me through the woods either. Hawkers should have been my only concern, but if the truth be known, I can't remember, ever so much as once, thinking on them. Coming upon a brook, I cleaned myself up as much as I could.

"I'd packed a bag with a few items I figured I might need, along with a fresh change of clothes before I'd left Pemberton. So wrapping my torn and bloody clothes around a rock, I threw it a good four or five feet out into the water and watched it sink out of sight. Now if I'd been anywhere near my home in Africa where I'd been born, I'd have had a pretty good idea of where I was and where I wanted to go. But standing there beside that brook, all I knew for sure was that Pemberton Plantation was somewhere behind me and that was the very last direction I intended on going. The light from the morning sun was about halfway up the trees on my right, and to this very day, I don't know why but I decided to go northeast. Most runaways set their goals on Ohio or Illinois, so I'd heard. Seems to me that area would be the place most Hawkers would be watching. So I kept the sun off my right shoulder, slowed my pace down considerably and stopped every hundred yards or so and gave a right good look see at what lay before me.

"Sometime around mid-morning I came upon an apple orchard. I guess I was at the far end of this orchard, because I could just about make out a house way off in the distance. Well, I sat myself down and watched that orchard for at least one hour based on how far the sun had moved overhead. After seeing no one in or anywhere around the orchard at all during this time, I finally stood up and began gathering apples which I stuffed in my bag. Reaching up and grabbing one more apple, I started chewing on it as I began walking again. I kept myself to the woods, although two or three times I came upon a dirt wagon road that appeared to be going in the direction I was going. The last thing I wanted was to be seen or confronted anywhere out in the open. So each time I came upon a road or pathway, I moved myself deeper into the woods to what I considered to be a safe distance away from it, all the time praying I wouldn't be seen.

"South Carolina is one strange place as far as I'm concerned. People call it the low country because much of it is swamp-like. It may be perfect for growing rice, but that's about all it's good for as far as I can see. During those next three days, my feet were constantly wet. That first day I actually took my shoes off and tying the laces, slung the shoes over my shoulder. My socks I laid over my shoulders also 'til the sun dried them out, then I put them in my bag. In the following days I noticed the land rising and most everywhere I stepped it was now dry. Sometime about the end of that first week I suspect I'd crossed over into North Carolina but I had no knowledge of this, not knowing a thing about the lay of the land. I'll not bore you with my doings the next week, only to say I stole a chicken from one farm I passed. At another place I managed to slip away with a peach pie I suspect some woman thought was safe as she had set it out on their side porch railing for cooling. Water was never a problem since brooks and streams were just about everywhere.

"As it happened, my first piece of good luck came in the form of a flat bottom boat, carrying assorted cargo and livestock, stuck solid on a sand bar. There were four men that I could see. Later I realized a fifth man was in the water on the opposite side of the boat. Now this stream wasn't fed by a tide, so no rising water could be counted upon coming to their rescue. They had tied two pigs together with a rope and cast them overboard hoping to lighten the boat's load. When this failed to make any difference, a crate standing about five feet tall was the next thing to go into the water. From where I stood, once this crate was thrown overboard, I noticed a slight rise of the boat off the sandbar. Looking ahead, I believed the sandbar fell off some and the water appeared to be a bit deeper four or five feet in front of the boat. About that time the two hogs came ashore not twenty feet from me. Glad to be out of the water, they rolled themselves in the sand while I walked over to them and without having the slightest bit of difficulty tied them to a tree.

"Meanwhile 'til this point I had not made myself known to those on the boat. But walking over and securing the hogs, suddenly all aboard the boat noticed me. Wading into the water, I reached the side of the boat within minutes."

'It appears you've some deeper water ten or twelve feet ahead of where you're stuck. And that last crate you threw overboard looked to me to have brought your boat a good inch or more up out of the sand. My guess is that if you tossed your anchor out ahead into the deeper water and you all got off the boat and into the water, you might just be able to pull this boat toward it and off this sandbar.' Simon looked each man in the eye to show he was not a threat to them.

"Well in less time than it's taken me to tell you all this, The boat was floating free once again and except for the hogs, whatever was inside that crate was back aboard safe. Now I was the one with a problem. These five men, all black themselves, were sure to be asking me questions I couldn't begin to think on how I'd answer. Where was I from? Was I a runaway or a free black? Was I alone? The tallest of the five, the man that had been in the water on the opposite side of the boat when I first came upon this scene, stepped off the boat into water that came up to his waist. In five or six steps he was standing before me, shaking my hand."

'You are truly a Godsend sent to us from above. Before you showed up we were talking about just what we'd do being stuck fast in that sand as we were. Now I'll tell you straight, I'm the only free Black on this boat. I've even got papers saying so, not that any Hawker, or possibly any white man would honor them. We're trying to make our way to Southport. I've a half-brother what lives there and owns a boat. Not a sorry flat bottom pretender to be a boat like this piece of junk we've been on. I'm talking a real ocean going boat that he's offered to take us all the way up to Connecticut on. He's slipped past more Yankee blockade boats than I'm told you can shake a stick at.

'He's originally from Nassau in the Bahamas. So even when he has been stopped at sea a couple of times, no one wants to mess with him. His boat is named the BAHAMA LADY and flies an English flag. I understand he has a wife and child in Southport, along with a wife and two children in Nassau. Mostly he hauls rum from the Islands up to Connecticut, or sometimes somewhere on Long Island. Now just what he returns to Nassau with I've never asked, never really wanted to know, and that's the God's honest fact.

'His name is Jean Baptiste. My name is John Reed, and being born and raised in the Bahamas I never was a slave. I don't speak like these other four, never having been anywhere near Africa. The papers I carry are stamped with the official English seal on them and written in what you'd call the King's English.'

"John stood just about the same height as me, and looking at the two of us one would think we could pass for brothers. Now as to these other four, John pointed at each of the men with him before speaking again."

'Silent, here, doesn't speak a word, not one. Seems he had something happen to him early on in life that left him speechless and he's been that way ever since. Tavernier came ashore down in the Key's somewhere near Key Largo. My guess is that since he landed there, that's the name given him and it stuck. Jose got his name while he was in Havana, Cuba. I guess the Spanish couldn't make hide nor hair out of his African name. Umba is another story for sure. Near as I can figure he was captured somewhere in Africa and eventually brought here and sold to a Plantation in Louisiana. Now whatever the hell he did there I've never learned. But if he wasn't wearing that shirt, which in over a month now I've only seen him take it off once, you might just throw-up. His back has been lashed so many times, I don't believe there is one square inch of clear, fresh skin visible.

'As I've said, we're hoping to get to Southport. From there these men are willing to go just about anywhere north: Rhode Island, Long Island, Connecticut, I truly mean anywhere just as its well north of here.'

"John then walked to where I had secured the pigs. Cutting the rope he watched them scamper off among the undergrowth. Saying that he suspected there would be dozens of pigs throughout this area in no time and that those two would only have just slowed us up if we'd have tried to keep them with us.

"For the next three days the six of us paddled and floated on that flat bottom boat so long as it was going east. On the fourth day the water we were on became more and more chocked with clumps of mangroves looking like little islands. Finally we forced the boat a good ten or twelve feet into a thick growth of interwoven mangrove. Taking whatever we could carry, John hacked several holes in the boat's bottom. The water wasn't more than four feet deep when we stepped out of the boat. What we took to be an island lay about a quarter mile northeast of the mangrove from where we stood. The water itself was a greenish blue. Later we learned that a twenty foot wide deep section of water lay between us and the land we intended crossing over to.

"While we were looking at this stretch of water we'd

have to cross, I noticed movement off to our left, 'Hawkers!' I whispered to my new found friends. 'I see at least three of them off to our left.'

"As I focused more, I could see at least three men appearing to be moving toward us. They moved slowly, and whenever they stopped they stepped behind trees shielding themselves from our view."

'They'll not be catching me,' Umba said as he dove headfirst into the water before him. With powerful strokes, he crossed the small river of water in less than two minutes. Exiting on the other side he looked back only once, then with a slight nod of his head to those he'd left behind, he quickly vanished among the palms that covered the far shore.

"John Reed looked at me and asked me what I thought of the situation. I told him that I saw that at least one of them had a gun, but I suspected that they all were armed. Escape appeared our only hope. I was for following Umba and crossing over this water as quickly as possible. Then I was for heading northeast as fast as these legs would carry me. But first I'd run straight east hoping they'd see me and try to track me in that direction."

John smiled at me and said, 'I don't really need to run, I'm a free man. Born in the Bahamas with papers to prove who I am and where I'm from. But I don't like Hawkers to a point where I don't really care if they live or die. I suspect that's the way they think about runaways also.'

At this point Tavernier and Silent slipped into the woods and began running south.

'It appears it's just you and me,' John said. 'I agree northeast is the direction we should aim for once we cross this water. Now I'm not being kindhearted, but once we're on the other side I intend on letting you run straight out. In my checkered past I did a lot of hunting. Never used a gun, and never really cared who owned the land I was on. I set snares for animals, and traps for humans. I'm thinking I can slow these Hawkers up some and maybe even put a hurt on one. That would be best, as whoever he's with will have to stop and help him. So you just be getting yourself across this spit of water and don't be thinking on looking back. I'll be doing what to my way of thinking I got to do in order to make these Hawkers give up the chase. I figure sometime about dark I'll be catching up with you, and together we'll continue on toward my brother's place.'

"I crossed the water and began running as soon as I felt dry land underfoot," Simon said. "Several times I intentionally broke limbs off small trees giving anyone following me the impression I'd passed that way in my escape attempt. When I believed most of a full hour had passed, I stopped and rested while leaning against a pine tree. When I'd recovered my breath sufficiently, I turned and moved off in the direction I suspected to be northeast. In a half hour I heard what eventually turned out to be the surf of the Atlantic Ocean off to my right. Moving in that direction, the ocean came into view within ten minutes. As sure as day follows night, I believed God had to be watching over me, because I soon learned I'd come upon the Atlantic Ocean not three miles south of our destination. Looking not fifty yards ahead, I saw John sitting upon a rock throwing stones at the incoming waves."

John smiled and jumped down from his perch upon the rock. 'My brother's place isn't far up this coast. I'm guessing two, three miles at the most from where we're standing. Those Hawkers had a terrible time back there,' he said. 'I counted four of them all together. But it appeared one tripped on a vine and fell on a sharpened piece of bamboo. Damned if it didn't go right through his leg and come out the other side. The last I saw of them, they had him upright with a man supporting each side of him. I was close enough to hear the other one bellyaching about the money they were losing letting us slip away." Looking up at the sky John said, 'It'll be dark soon. I say we get a move on and head to my brother's place while it's still light.'

Chapter 2
Freedom Becomes Possible

"Jean Baptiste stood a good three inches taller than his half-brother John," Simon said. "I'd figured John at just about one hundred pounds, maybe a touch more. Jean doubled his half-brother in weight, but moved easily while constantly smiling. Jean also had that sing-song like voice of the Islands."

'You be damn lucky you showed up today I can tell you that for sure,' Jean said grinning from ear to ear. 'Tomorrow I sail home to the Bahamas. Then once I've everything aboard that I need and spent a night with my wife, I'll point my BAHAMA LADY toward somewhere in New England. Maybe I'll try Rhode Island first? But then again Long Island has always been lucky for me. I'm always thinking that someday if I get myself a Frenchman aboard that I can trust, I just might try to keep going north and attempt to establish a base of trade somewhere in Canada. I'm hearing they have some extra pretty women in Canada. After such a long voyage, I'd be ready to bed down with a pretty French woman or two. But only after I've settled on a guarantee of future business. For me, business comes first. Although in my time I'll admit one or two, maybe three women have taken my mind off business, letting pleasure come first.'

Then turning to his brother, Jean asked, 'You said there might be two men and I see only this one fellow?'

I stepped forward and said, 'Umba was very nervous and once I mentioned seeing Hawkers, Umba decided to return to the woods and continue on alone.'

'That was very foolish of him,' Jean said. 'North Carolina will be hard to cross through, but nothing compared with Virginia. Many people in both places will turn him in to collect a reward. With us he had a chance. Alone I give him one, maybe two days at most, before he is caught.

'Well now it is dark enough that we can go into my house. John, I will bed you down at the house, your friend we'll take right to the boat and he can sleep safe there. I doubt anyone will come to my house tonight, but if someone did, I could explain your being there with my wife and children. Simon will be safe on the BAHAMA LADY tonight. No one would dare go near my boat no matter if I were there or not there. I figure to set sail early tomorrow. Tomorrow morning we'll take your friend a hot breakfast down from my house when we go to the boat.'

"Dawn had barely broken when Jean and John arrived at the BAHAMA LADY. For minutes they thought I had abandoned the boat as they saw no sign of me. Then the tarp covering a skiff at the rear of the boat moved and I ever so slowly crawled out of the skiff and onto the main deck. Jean laughed watching me twist and turn as I worked the kinks out of my body."

'Here! I've brought you some hot coffee with maybe just a small touch of rum in it.' Jean said. 'My wife also made you some clam fritters for your breakfast. Eat them while they're still nice and warm. You tend to your breakfast while we prepare the LADY for setting sail.' Within minutes two men came walking along the wharf and threw their stuffed canvas bags aboard the BAHAMA LADY prior to stepping onto the main deck.

'I smell rum,' the thinnest of the two said within seconds of his bare feet touching the decking of the ship. 'And what's with these other two we've got aboard?'

'Someday young Pape here will be a captain of his own boat for sure. Not much gets past his eyes or nose, that's why I've had him sailing with me for these past four or five years,' Jean said. 'Now Paul Barlow, standing beside Pape, came to the Bahamas from St. Thomas five years ago. I believe I was the very first person on the island he met. He'd sailed a twenty-foot sailboat there from St. Thomas, so I knew right away he knew his way around a boat and around the sea. As time goes on, he may or may not tell you why he left his home on St. Thomas, but that's not for me to say, so I'll leave it up to him. Soon after meeting him, I talked him into coming with me to my home here in North Carolina. Since then he's been here with me a few times. He is a good man that I can trust.'

Jean turned from Pape and Paul and pointed at his half-brother John. 'I believe John has spent his whole life ashore, and if so we'll be finding that out soon enough. This other fellow is called Simon and I've been told he just up and walked away from a plantation down in South Carolina. Right now he's looking to land himself somewhere safe up north. Now that rum, you smell Pape, is a very slight addition I added to Simon's coffee. We've barrels of its like we'll be storing down below once we reach Nassau. But as has always been the rule aboard the BAHAMA LADY, not a bit of that rum will be tasted until after it's ashore up north and I've been paid my asking price.' Jean wetted his finger and held it up in the air. 'We've got the wind at our backside, so I suggest in the strongest way that we cast off immediately. We've several days ahead of us to figure out just who is who, and who knows what about sailing.'

Simon took a sip of water, wiped his mouth with the back of his hand and smiled. "Now I know your dying to have me tell you about Darlene, and I promise you I will. But several things happened before her and I met up following my leaving the plantation.

"First off we sailed for Jean's home in the Bahamas. After a couple of days spent there getting the BAHAMA LADY fully loaded and ready to sail to New England, we finally set sail from the Bahamas. We were a little over four weeks before we saw the shoreline of Long Island. Some days we'd be sailing North, when for reasons I know nothing of, Jean would turn us somewhat around and we'd sail for most of a full day East. Then he'd turn the BAHAMA LADY North again and this time for maybe a full two days he'd have us holding steady, pointed North. I will tell you that in all that time at sea I only saw one other ship. And on only one day did we have rain. As God is my witness, I never once got sea sick.

"I tell you this because John had one horrible day along about our third day after leaving the Bahamas. We were clipping along quite fast, and the front of the boat kept rising and then quickly falling back into the sea with a smacking sound. When it did this, everything on the boat either swayed side to side, or pitched up and down. Pape and Paul didn't even seem to notice anything wrong. Jean just smiled and went about the business of commanding his ship. I admit that I held onto one thing or another just to keep my footing. But my stomach was fine and I actually enjoyed it when the salt spray off the ocean swept over the side and fell against me.

"But John was a different story. I've seen sick men before, but none to compare with poor John. Within the first hour he'd fouled all his clothes. He'd thrown up in a bucket, but that proved difficult as sometimes just when he was throwing up the ship would rise up on a wave and the bucket would slide down along the decking causing him to throw up into the scupper running along the full length of the boat. That night John had recovered and put all his soiled clothes in a clean bucket of sea water. John had Paul start a fire going in the galley and within the hour we were enjoying our supper.

"Now there is an interesting thing I learned that evening while enjoying that conk chowder. Seems back during America's Revolution against England, England decided to tax the people on the islands of the Bahamas also. Well the people of the islands would have no part of having their food and goods most of which they imported from England taxed. Since they were in no condition to actually go to war with England, they just stopped importing everything from England.

"The islands have thousands of Conk throughout their waters, so they went about learning how to cook and eat it. Pretty soon Conk became a food staple of the islands. Better yet, it spread to the other islands also. I'm told they came up with about thirty different ways to prepare Conk, and it also became something of a cash crop for the islanders.

"Well back to my story. A few weeks later we landed at a small fishing village in Rhode Island called Wickford that, I was told, was settled in the early 1700's. This is where Jean sold five barrels of rum to the first merchant he'd spoken with. That night we stayed ashore and enjoyed a fine meal of Haddock and potatoes while listening to some very good music. At dawn the following day, we were off headed north once again. Six days later we tied up at a long dock in New Bedford. Less than ten years earlier New Bedford was the whaling capital of New England. It was also one of the richest cities in the east. Whaling ships were still sailing out of

New Bedford when we arrived there, but the industry had slowed down considerably.

"Drilled oil was quickly replacing the need for whale sperm oil, and it burned cleaner and cost less. Plus those drilling for oil didn't have to contend with the unpredictable seas, or the four or more years New Bedford men were forced to spend aboard ship and away from home in order to fill their many empty casks with whale oil. New Bedford was a mixture of the old and the new. If Mystic Connecticut was the holy ground of whaling, New Bedford represented the nitty gritty underbelly of the whaling industry. And it was in the taverns and brothels of this underbelly that men, such as Jean Baptiste, increased their fortune. A barrel of rum might sell for three times the value here in New Bedford that it would command in Rhode Island or out on Long Island.

"Now I was getting to the point where I'd had enough of sailing. I was well north now, and felt safe regarding being captured as an escaped slave from South Carolina. John Reed had taken a real true liking to me, and spent considerable time with me explaining exactly where we were, and the distances and directions to places like Providence and Boston. And it was on our last day in New Bedford before we set sail for Long Island that John took me aside and handed me his own papers showing he was a free man born in the Bahamas. As he handed me the papers, he said, 'You may just have need of these someday. I myself can't picture anyone ever confronting me, or questioning where I was born or came from. Nowhere on this paper does it say black or white. Plus if need be, I can always get myself a new copy when I'm back in Nassau. So now you are John Reed if anyone should ever ask.'

"Jean took up a collection on behalf of the crew, and handed me almost twenty dollars. The following morning I walked along the pier following the BAHAMA LADY as she made her way out to sea once again. At the end of the pier I actually wiped tears from my eyes. I was no longer and never again would be a slave. I was in the north and had money in my pocket that was my own. As I watched the BAHAMA LADY moving further and further away, I finally turned and walked back along the length of the dock and into the town."

'This be your lucky day mate,' a tall sailor, wearing cut off pants that ended just above his knees and a blue and white shirt which appeared much like the sailor – neither had seen water or soap in more than a month, said as he slapped Simon on his shoulder. They stood in the street in front of a bar that held a sign telling everyone it was the Mariner. Looking up Simon could plainly see a harpooned whale weathervane on its roof.

'I saw you watching your ship sailing away and figured right off that you'd be a prime seaman, just the kind Captain Martin would be looking to take aboard his ship the PROVIDENCE.' The sailor pointed over his shoulder toward the bar and said, 'Why don't you and I go inside and have ourselves a drink while we talk.' To say the inside of the barroom was just dirty would be doing it a justice far much more that it deserved. Only seven tables stood, or in one case leaned, against the wall available to serve customers. A staircase led to the second floor where in six small separate rooms ladies of the night plied their profession.

'Now Captain Martin is quite well known here in New Bedford, and the PROVIDENCE has never yet returned without it having a full cargo of whale oil aboard,' Davy Jones said. 'Why I've seen hands walk off the PROVIDENCE with as much as 1/7th of the silver in their pocket earned once the cargo had been inspected and the money divided up according to the rules of the business. By the by, my name is Jones and I guess you could consider me Captain Martin's right hand man, that would be following Thomas Knot, of course, who's first mate aboard the PROVIDENCE.'

Before he said another word, Mary Beck walked over to the table and addressed Davy Jones, 'Beer, Rum or Whiskey, Davy? While I've plenty of all on hand, the three of us will be seeing your money on this table before I'll be wasting my time fetching drinks you hope to be putting on account, which I can tell you straight out won't be happening.' Mary stood just under five feet tall, but sticking out of her apron in plain sight was a belaying pin she'd used many times on sailors the likes of Davy Jones. Her hair was red, cut short so it ended at the sides just above her ears. Her blouse was buttoned right up to her neckline. 'I'll not be flaunting my fleshy treasures, or going upstairs entertaining the likes of what comes in here, I can promise you that!' she said. Instead of a skirt Mary wore black leather pants. And backing up her belaying pin, from a belt she wore holding her pants up, she had an eight inch dagger in a brown leather sheath.

Davy Jones pushed his chair back and stood up. 'Well there's more decent places in this town for a sailorman to enjoy a drink and not be insulted before his guest by a woman what doesn't know her place and that's for certain sure.' Motioning to Simon to follow him, he started for the front door. Turning and seeing Simon still sitting in his chair Davy hollered, 'I hope you're pleased with yourself, Mary. I'll be telling Captain Martin how you treat customers what foolishly come into this tavern.' In seconds he'd slammed the door behind him and was gone.

'Is Davy Jones a friend of yours?' Mary asked.

'Shaking my head, I chuckled, 'Actually, I met him on the dock not ten minutes ago. Didn't even know his name until we'd sat down here at this table. I'm sure he was hoping to get me to sign on to a whaling ship, but not in his lifetime would I ever consider doing so. And as far as a whaling ship is concerned, I've never been on one. I sailed from the Bahamas with a friend who does business selling rum and such hereabout in New England. That one sailing convinced me that keeping my feet on dry land was the proper way the Lord intended me to live out my years.'

'I've just made some chowder, and if I say so myself it's

the best you'll taste in all of Massachusetts,' Mary said. 'How about a bowl and a drink on me while we sit here and chat? Look at this place, almost noon and not a soul inside but us two. Even the girls what keep the upstairs rooms going are all off somewhere.' Standing she asked once again about a bowl of chowder and this time I smiled and said yes.

'You very well may have sailed here from the Bahamas,' Mary said as they sat eating the chowder. 'But I suspect it was more of a roundabout trip that landed you here in New Bedford. Now don't go giving a tinker's damn regarding my wondering where your journey actually began. I'm a strict abolitionist. I don't give a hoot about those that think otherwise. I just want this bloody foolish war over, and each and every man and woman that walks upon our soil to be free. I'd guess you're ailing in your brain if New Bedford is your destination. As for me and were I you, I'd be planning once this day is done to be thinking hard on heading elsewhere.'

"I guess you could say Mary had me over a barrel." Simon said. "She'd figured me out already and made it plain that what she thought about my past didn't matter. And she hadn't lied about that chowder either. I can tell you that I've never had the like of it since, and would gladly give whatever amount was asked for another heaping bowl of it.

"Mary also suggested I leave New Bedford once we'd finished our lunch. She let me out the back way, just in case Davy hadn't given up on getting me as a new shipmate. She'd seen him take money out of many a poor man's pocket to pay their bill, then just about carry them out of here no doubt straight to the ship PROVIDENCE.

"It was just a little past full noon when I set my sights on Fall River and began walking west." Simon said. "Actually Providence, Rhode Island was my goal as I set out from New Bedford. I guess I thought a thousand times during that trek to Providence, how I should have just stayed right in that small village in Rhode Island when I'd first landed aboard the BAHAMA LADY. But then I'd have missed out on meeting Mary along with all the other things I experienced having continued on to New Bedford."

"After two hours of walking, a man and his wife came along in a wagon drawn by two horses and offered me a lift. That wagon was filled with sacks of wheat, and it didn't take me five minutes to work my body down among those sacks and fall fast asleep. I finally woke up when we were less than two miles from Fall River."

'You sure was tired when you climbed into this wagon,' the lady said as she smiled at me. 'Jake and I, Jake's my husband,' she said while putting her arm around his shoulder. 'Well, we figured to just let you sleep until your body figured it was time for you to wake up.

'We've an hour, maybe a little less, before we get to Fall River. We make this trip every two weeks, and this is the very first time we've ever stopped and given someone a ride. But Jake saw you shuffling along and weaving a slight bit from side to side, he figured before long you'd just fall down and go to sleeping right where you lay in the road, or even maybe you'd roll yourself over into the ditch. Jake couldn't let that happen, so that's why he stopped and offered you to come along with us.

'Sara is my name and I have to tell you, Jake told me you'd be asleep before we went a full mile.' Saying this, Sara laughed. 'Married twenty-six years to this man, and I've never known him to be wrong before. But this time I'm thinking he was off by fully half a mile.'

"Are you ever going to get back to Darlene?" Jessie asked once again, as she shifted her position in the chair.

"Now we're not all that far off coming to what I suspect you consider the meat of the matter. I'll be running into Darlene in Providence, Rhode Island, and I'll even skip over most of what took place between Fall River and Providence just so as to keep you from pestering me about Darlene again." Simon laughed.

Chapter 3
The Past Returns

"I landed in Providence, Rhode Island about a full month after leaving the BAHAMA LADY. I've got to tell you, I came across some mighty pretty country during that bit of travel. It was just before I arrived in Providence that I heard the war had finally ended. General Lee had surrendered to General Grant some place down in Virginia. Now I'd be lying if I said I wasn't thinking about Master Jonathan and those people still down there on the Pemberton Plantation. Master Jonathan was a right fair and proper man. His overseer also really cared for the slaves at that plantation although he never did take a shine or anything you'd call a liking to me. I swear to God, you could ask each and every slave at Pemberton, and you'd not hear one bad word regarding either of them." Simon reached over, took another sip of the water and set the glass back on the table.

"Providence appeared to me to be a right busy place. I'd never seen so many wagons and such in the streets anywhere before I arrived in Providence," Simon said. "People were real friendly also. Seldom did a person pass me by that didn't say

'Hi', or 'good day.' My being black didn't seem to call for any special notice from what I could see.

"Now Main Street was rutted-up some, and there were horse droppings here and there also, as was to be expected. But the side streets I saw were mostly as clean as a whistle. I have to believe the people living in their fine houses along the side streets not only picked up any debris they found lying about, I actually saw a man out in front of his house using a rake and smoothing out the dirt on the road.

"I heard the east side of Providence had its dark side. Ships of all sizes tied up at the docks that lined the river over there. I also was told that there were at least two taverns on each block along the waterfront. I never did get down to the waterfront or even over anywhere near the east side.

"Walking up Main Street, I came upon the Jefferson Hotel. Right next door to the hotel was a decent size restaurant called "Clem's Lobster Kettle". As I stood looking at the place, I heard a voice say, 'Simon, step on up and sit yourself down next to me.' Well I'll be damned, as true as I'm sitting here in this office I couldn't believe my eyes, but there sat Darlene looking right at me. There was a porch that ran all across the front of this restaurant, and then continued down the side of the building facing the hotel. There were about eight tables on the front section of this porch and there, big as life, sat Darlene. I finally came to my senses and walked up the steps, then turned and walked to the table Darlene was sitting at."

'Sit yourself down and take a load off your feet,' she said while pointing to a chair just to her left. Before I could say a word, Darlene told me she and Jonathan were divorced. 'I left Pemberton at Jonathan's request, about three weeks after you'd run away.' Darlene said. 'I don't know if you know it or not, but Jonathan never did put out a run-away notice regarding you. It's funny in a way, I was so caught up being in love with Alex since I was a child, and I don't believe that I ever really gave my marriage to Jonathan a chance to succeed. Then later, after the war ended I learned that Alex had died at the battle of Petersburg.

'Anyway, the day Jonathan returned from Richmond, James Temper told him everything he knew regarding you and me and our being suspected lovers. Jonathan never even raised his voice when he came into my room and confronted me. He said he was going to divorce me and offered to buy me a house anywhere in Charleston, or he'd give me the amount of money he'd have spent on buying me a house and I could do with it whatever I chose. He told me I had one hour to gather my things, and then he wanted me off the property. I spent exactly the rest of that one day in Charleston, never looked at any houses and left for Savannah the very next day. That one day I spent in Charleston is a day I shall never forget. The people apparently knew or thought they knew all that had gone on while I was at Pemberton. They were outwardly cruel and downright rude to me. It was disgusting! I'd had people whisper and say things behind my back in the past, but that day the people, the women mostly, were just plain outright nasty.'

Darlene stopped speaking and caught the attention of a waiter. 'You simply must order yourself a meal while we talk', she said to me. 'Now the meal is on me, and I won't even listen to the word "no" coming from you. Glory be, but I'm thrilled to see you, and I don't care if we sit here until the moon comes up, or the owner directs us to leave. I want to hear about everything you've done since you ran away from the plantation, and how it is you've ended up here in Providence.'

Taking Darlene's advice, I ordered some clam cakes and a glass of local beer. In what seemed like only minutes, the waiter brought a plate filled with six steaming hot clam cakes, plus a tall glass of beer which he set down in front of me, then without saying anything except "enjoy", he returned inside the restaurant.

'I've had rum when I was aboard the BAHAMA LADY, but this will be my first time drinking beer,' I told Darlene. 'You know, I never gave a thought to food before I ran away from Pemberton. Only when I got so hungry that it hurt, then I thought about food.'

Simon bit into the first clam cake, then lifted the glass and took a small drink of the beer. For several seconds he remained looking down at the plate, then he looked up and smiled. Lifting the glass of beer once again he took another drink, this time taking in two or three times the amount he'd first sampled. 'This is very good,' he said looking at Darlene. 'Not just the beer, but the cake has a nice filling in it that pleases me.'

"Well, Darlene and I really did sit right there until it was obvious the owner intended closing up for the day," Simon said. "Less than a block away was a small park with nice benches and beautiful big trees that allowed the moonlight to shine through on us," Simon continued. "Later as we sat there I told her my story and even showed her the paper saying that I was John Reed, a free black, born in the Bahamas.

"I mentioned the flat bottom boat stuck on the sandbar, and the men I met when I helped them free the boat. I said that I'd sailed on a boat called the BAHAMA LADY from North Carolina to the Bahamas, and then on to New England. I told her how I was almost shanghaied in New Bedford and would have no doubt been taken aboard a whaling ship if it wasn't for the kindness of a bar maid named Mary, who fed me, let me out the back door of the tavern telling me to get as far away from New Bedford, and do so as fast as possible. Between walking and getting a ride in a wagon, I ended up in a place called Fall River.

"Now I don't know why. Maybe it was my first landing in Rhode Island back in Wickford while I was aboard the BAHAMA LADY with John Reed that got me to thinking of going back there. But you know, the people I saw there in that small village all seemed so nice. The town itself was really very pretty. The land where we docked stuck out so there was water on both sides where boats could tie up. A small fish shop was at the end of the land so the people in boats could just stop there and buy bait or food before they went home, or out fishing.

"John and I had walked up the narrow street to where it met with a larger main street. All this time I was pushing a wheel barrow filled with five kegs of rum covered over with a tarp from the boat. Anyway, John did his dickering with a restaurant owner there, and before I knew it we was walking back to the BAHAMA LADY with me now pushing an empty wheelbarrow. But for whatever the reason, when I left Fall River I set my mind on coming back to Rhode Island. Now what tomorrow holds in store for me I haven't a clue. Maybe I'll go back to that small village and try to make myself a life there."

Darlene just sat there and smiled for a bit before talking. 'As I've said, I spent just one ungodly day in Charleston. A carriage was leaving for Savannah early the following morning and I made damn sure I was on it. I stayed in Savannah for two full months, which looking back upon that period I've come to realize just how much it changed, and no doubt saved me.

'I wrote Jonathan a short letter asking him for one thousand dollars. I said I'd seen a house in Charleston, but just couldn't abide living in that city, the people there all being so against me. I gave him an address in Savannah to forward the money to me. Well Jonathan sent me five hundred dollars which I realized was really more than fair, everything considered. I stayed in Savannah about another full month working as a waitress at a fairly nice restaurant down on the waterfront.

'It was about the end of that month when I realized I'd stopped drinking and hadn't used laudanum or any other drugs since I'd left Pemberton. I actually began feeling good about myself, and at the same time realized that the Confederacy was finished. I figured once this war was over Northerners would be coming down South Lording it over anyone living here.

'My being a white female and having been a slave owner on a large plantation, well the pictures of how I believed I'd be treated that took form in my mind told me it was time for me to leave the South. I made my way up through Maryland, and if I say so myself, I doubt I'd spent more than ten dollars getting that far north. Eventually I ended up here in Providence.

'I swear I've lost at least ten pounds since I'd left Savannah. Now I'm working at a small woman's shop not two blocks from here, which works out perfectly for me. I end up paying less than half price for the clothes I buy, and I've limited myself to one real meal a day. I say one real meal because I'm not above enjoying a free coffee of a morning with possibly two or three little cakes Margaret the owner brings into the shop each day.

'I can't say how long I'll stay here in Providence, but the more I think on it, I'd like to start a new life, a really new life, possibly somewhere out west. The hotel next door has some of the most interesting and beautiful paintings that were painted out west. And I've talked with several people who have actually been out there, or have friends that have been there. Most seem to start their journey at St. Joseph in Missouri. Now from what I've learned speaking to several people that should know, St. Joseph appears to be almost half the way across this country.

'I even stopped in at a school house one day as the children were coming out, and the teacher was nice enough to roll out a map of this country showing me all the places I'd have to cross over just to reach what was considered the starting point for going out west. That teacher's name was James and I understand he was married. But believe me, that didn't stop him one minute from looking my body over from head to toe and making me feel like I was naked. Well I finally thanked him for showing me the map, and got myself back outside in the sunlight quick as I could. Providence is really something ahead of its time when I come to think about it. Why down south I'd seldom if ever heard of a man being a school teacher. Then I came to learn that Providence had several woman doctors also. Well it was enough to make my head spin.'

Simon just smiled and nodded his head listening to Darlene. 'You know something,' Simon said. 'I got to thinking that is why the South never had a chance of winning the war. Everywhere I've looked in Fall River and in most every large town I'd come through there were factories. Mostly two or three story brick buildings where inside they were making most anything a person could imagine. And unlike the South where for the most part the women stayed right to home, up North many of the people working in those factories were either women or in some cases even children. Why right here in Rhode Island they made more for their soldiers in a day than the south could manage to turn out in two weeks. I'm talking blankets, stretchers, crutches and such like. Then when I got to really thinking about it, I realized the ones that were making blankets were also making uniforms for their soldiers, along with nice clothes for the folks living locally. The ones making crutches were also making all kinds of furniture at the same time. Now I know men on both sides were dying in the war and that was terrible. People down south were also often searching out food for a decent meal.

'But up north here, folks were doing quite well for themselves. When I first started running away from the plantation, I saw buildings that were being knocked down or just plain blown apart when they were caught in the crossfire of the war. But look around us here. Look at the new houses and businesses that appear to have been built in the past few years. I've heard people say it'll take years for the South to get itself back to where it was before the war. Now with the war ended I suspect the North will prosper even better than before.

'During those first days as I ran north, some days I ate some days I didn't. One day I gathered apples from some person's orchard, and these lasted me three or four days. Another time I stole a chicken and cooked it over a small fire I'd started. I managed to swipe a pie a lady had set out on her porch railing to cool. I'd never had food from a can before, but once I got on the BAHAMA LADY it seems that every day we'd eat something out of a can.

'Jean Baptiste who owned the BAHAMA LADY, I'd guess he had almost fifty cans of food aboard that boat when we sailed bound for New England. Some of those cans held meat, while others had fish in them. He also had a large ice bucket filled with jerked chicken. You tell me you've cut down to one real meal a day. I can tell you that when you are running like when I was running away from the plantation, food and eating were a long way from my mind. Only when I got so hungry that it hurt, then I thought about food.'

'So what are your plans now?' Darlene asked.

'I'd be bald-faced lying to you,' Simon answered, 'if I said I actually had a plan in mind for what I'll do, or where I'll be going. One thing I know for sure, I have no intention of returning to Africa. I told you I've given some thought to returning to that small village in Rhode Island where we'd first come ashore when I was sailing in the BAHAMA LADY. Then again everything is so new to me that I just don't honestly know which way I'll jump.

'You are the first person I've heard mention going out west, and I'm sure I'll be giving that idea some thought now also. As for me, talking with John Reed and several other people I've met, I've considered continuing north, possibly all the way up into Canada. But in the back of my mind I seem to keep thinking about the weather. Now I've never seen ice like I understand they have here sometime in the winter. Most parts of Canada I'm told most of the year is covered with snow.' Simon smiled and made his body shiver. 'These African bones are telling me that right here is possibly as far north as I should be thinking of going. Now, as for out west, I'll have to do some thinking on that for sure.'

'Well for right now, I'd best be getting back to my room behind the shop,' Darlene said. 'I know a store owner just down the street from the shop I work at that is looking for help. If you'd like, I could introduce you to him tomorrow. Maybe he'd even have a place where you could sleep, or at least know of somewhere available. I quit work at three every afternoon, I'd be glad to meet you outside the Lobster Kettle and take you to meet him.'

'I will be sitting right there on the front porch of the Lobster Kettle tomorrow when you get out of work.' Simon said.

Then he watched her walk along the pathway and eventually out of sight. Later sitting alone on that park bench he thought of all he and Darlene had talked about. Within minutes his head was filled with thoughts of out west, Canada, possibly staying right here and finding a job, or maybe even going back to that little town in Rhode Island where he'd first come ashore.

He also thought about Darlene. She was not the Darlene he remembered from the plantation. There was now a sadness, and yet a gentleness, about Darlene. He also wondered how things were back at Pemberton Plantation since the war was over and the slaves had all been made free. Where were all those people now, and what had happened to Jonathan? Before he realized it a Constable was tapping a nightstick against his knee. Simon had fallen asleep and was startled by the touch of the policeman's club.

'You can't sleep here in this park,' the Constable said.

'I am sorry sir,' Simon said. 'I was talking with a friend, and then after she left I was sitting here just thinking and I must have fallen asleep.'

'And I'm thinking you are a newcomer here in Providence. Well let me lay down a piece or two of our laws regarding this here park. Although we've no gate or wall as you can see, no one is allowed in this park after ten at night. Now it's plain to see you're not drinking and don't appear to have any alcohol about you, and it's lucky for you that your lady friend isn't here with you either. There are any number of places here about, taverns and such like where men and women can entertain themselves to their hearts delight. I'll be telling you that along about eleven each night I take a walk through this park. I trust I'll not be finding you sleeping on a bench here in the future.'

That night Darlene lay awake thinking of everything she and Simon had said. She also admitted to herself that she still held a special place in her heart for Simon. Thinking of Jonathan, she wondered if she went back to Pemberton and spoke with him, telling him how she really felt regarding the period when they had been married, and how badly she now realized that she, and she alone, was responsible for the way their marriage ended.

She wondered if somehow the past between them could be locked away and maybe, just maybe they could put together a good and decent life for their future. This very night as she looked up at the ceiling and pulled the covers up closer to her chin, for the first time she admitted to herself that she actually did love Jonathan.

It wasn't with the passion she'd loved Simon, and as for Alex, he'd been little more than a childhood love from beginning to end. He'd been her Knight in shining armor since she had been a little girl. The castle they would live in, the coach and four that would take them to so many magical places. Although only a figment of her imagination, these things were to her as real as the make believe tea she pretended to pour as she had done so often as a child while she'd sat at a small table across from her doll.

Simon walked out of the park and down along the road that went past Clem's Lobster Kettle. Providence was the biggest city he had ever been in, and from a small rise on the road where he stood, looking what he considered North West, he could see the city stretch out before him for what appeared to be over a mile. Two blocks further on, he saw a large church. When he arrived at it, he was in total awe of the building. He counted twenty-two stone steps leading up to large double doors at the front entrance to the church. At each side of the building stone towers containing bells reached up toward the heavens more than doubling the height of the main building.

Slowly he climbed the steps finally reaching the church doors. He was surprised to find them unlocked, and so he opened the one on the right side and entered the building. Fifty rows of pews led down toward the front of the church. Down nearer the alter, although it was now past mid-night, some candles still burned. The dim light they cast coupled with the light of the moon outside revealed to him that the windows along both walls were of beautiful stained glass, the first he had ever seen.

Taking a seat in the rear pew of the church, he inspected every inch of the interior of this building. Several statues stood throughout the Church. Knowing nothing of the religion on display here, he promised himself that he would return during a day when he hoped he could learn more about the church and the religion. As he sat there in that stone church looking up at the ceiling that arched far above his head, he thought back to his home in Africa.

His father's house in their village was round and made of mud and sticks. He remembered there were possibly twenty or twenty-five such houses that made up the village. Completely surrounding all these houses was a wall of brush standing shoulder high to the taller men of the village. This brush was laced with thorns and secured to the ground insuring that none but the biggest animals could break their way through into the center of the village.

A river ran freely within sight of this enclosed compound, and it was here the women went to wash clothes or secure water for their family's needs. He remembered also that at least three or four times each year, crocodiles would carry off a person at the water's edge who was not paying attention to their surroundings.

It was the same with hunting. Men from his village would arm themselves with spears and bows, and venture out looking to kill wild game in order to provide meat for the people of the village. Sometimes the hunt would be successful, sometimes not. And then there were times when those who went out hunting returned, but without one or two of their men. He, himself, had been captured by men from a different tribe. For several days he'd been tied to other captured men and women and forced to walk for miles until he finally saw the ocean for the first time in his life.

Simon stood up and slowly walked down the center isle of the church, all the time thinking of his past. He remembered being in the slave house at Pemberton on a night much like this. There the one window at each side of the house which was nothing more than an open square. A piece of wood secured by a length of rope lay below each of these windows upon the dirt or wood floor depending on the cabin. On pleasant nights the wood would be removed and the night air would circulate throughout the cabin. If it was raining or snowing, the wood would be lifted and fit into the window-opening keeping the weather out. At the time he'd considered the slave quarters at Pemberton a vast improvement over his father's house in Africa.

Now he stood in a world he did not understand. Men had been paid to build this beautiful church. They had bought their food at places such as the Lobster Kettle, or cooked their food at home having bought the food from one of the many shops he'd seen as he'd walked through the different towns he'd passed through since arriving in Rhode Island.

Stopping and standing still, he looked all around him at this beautiful building. Slowly raising his hands, he placed his fists against each side of his head. He knew standing here tonight, in this church, that he would never, ever fully understand life, or even his fellow man. In his mind the difference between his home in Africa and standing here were more than just worlds apart.

Turning, he walked to the rear of the church, opened the door and stepped outside. Quickly he descended the stone stairs. Without looking back at the church, Simon walked toward the Lobster Kettle. Coming upon a bench beside the walkway just short of being within sight of the restaurant, he sat down and within minutes once again fell asleep. The following day he met Darlene as planned and she introduced him to a Mr. Jordan Palm.

Chapter 4
Grit and Choices

'I've a wood working shop just a spit from where we're standing. I opened my shop ten years ago, and today I've enough business to keep three men working full time five days a week. Problem is I've only got two men presently. Now I'll be honest with you, Darlene is a good friend, and I'd do just about anything to please her. She tells me you're a fine upright fellow who needs a job and a place to stay. But right off I see three strikes against you.

'First off you're black! Don't get me wrong, I've always been against slavery, and I'm not holding your color against you. But I suspect because of your past, you can't read or write? I'm wondering if I was to hire you I'd possibly have to hire another fellow just to watch over you and explain each job I'd be assigning you. Then again I could just hire a young fellow graduating from St. Leo's that can both read and write, and with any luck I'd have myself a good worker that could settle himself fully into the trade in a month or two. As for needing a place to stay, this just seems to me to be another obstacle to my hiring you. Simon, I'm afraid I'm going to have to say, "No!" in regards to employing you. Believe me, I do sincerely wish it was the other way around. But I need someone now, and that someone whoever he might be has to be ready to step into my shop and go right to work on day one.'

Later Darlene and Simon sat on the porch at the Lobster Kettle and talked. Simon didn't appear depressed in the least over not being hired. 'I know I'll do alright, and I don't believe it will take all that long for me to find my way here in Providence.'

He told her about the church he'd visited, and that led to him also talking about his village in Africa, along with his time at Pemberton Plantation. 'I don't believe I'm here in Providence by accident, just as I don't believe my being at Pemberton was ever meant to be forever. And I'm not saying Providence is going to be the answer either. I do know a thing or two for sure though. I know I need to go someplace with you and make love with you again.

'And I know I'm not made for sleeping on park benches. So sometime today or at the latest by tomorrow, I'll find myself a room I can rent. Then before another week is over, I'll have myself a job. At Pemberton I rarely worked in the field. Blue had me working everywhere on that plantation. And I did so many different jobs that needing to read wasn't necessary. I remember building half of the horse barn, even cutting in new rafters by myself. My hands were also all over the blacksmith shop and I've mixed mortar and set brick.'

Simon smiled at Darlene and said, 'I bet you don't know half of what I know about horses. Many nights I'd saddle a horse from the barn and ride out back at the plantation. Once I had a horse throw a shoe and Blue taught me how to replace it. He was the only one who knew I had a mind of my own.' Simon looked around making sure no one was watching him, then he reached over and took Darlene's hand in his and kissed it. 'That day you caught me swimming when I was supposed to be taking the worn tools to the blacksmith shop, you have no idea how proud of myself I was as you looked at me. I came so close to telling you how wonderful the water felt and for a minute there I knew no fear of you.

'So for now I think we each should order some chowder and a beer. I've money to pay for our meal.' Letting go of Darlene's hand, he turned and called the owner over and ordered their meals.

The following day Simon found a small two room apartment quite by accident. As he walked along a street, he saw a man fall on his front lawn. The man had been weeding along his flowerbed and dropped his rake. Reaching down for it he'd lost his balance and fallen. The man was not hurt, but could not stand back up without help. Simon helped him up and then reached back down and picked up the rake.

'It's gotten so my legs just don't have the strength they use to have. Hell, a year ago this never would have happened. I am grateful for your helping me.' he said. 'My name is Mathew Johnson but everyone calls me Matt. I've lived right here most of my life with my wife Sara. She died a little over a year ago, so that's why now I'm doing the weeding and trying to keep up with her flowers. How about we go sit on the porch for a bit so I can catch my breath again?'

Matt and Simon talked for over an hour. Simon said he was looking for employment, along with his need for an apartment. Matt mentioned having a spare room he'd be willing to rent, while Simon offered to help with the weeding once he found employment provided the job he ended up with allowed him enough free time to help Matt in anything Matt felt needed doing around the house that was presently beyond his doing. Simon left Matt sitting there on the porch saying he'd be back as soon as he'd found employment and had money to pay whatever rent Matt would be asking.

The following day Simon walked into Mr. Jordan Palm's woodworking shop. 'You know, being able to read and write must be wonderful. But although I can do neither, I've built buildings, worked with animals and I'd be shocked if you're doing something in this shop that I couldn't figure out and do well even without being able to read. You said you needed a man that could step right in, or that you could hire someone right out of school that within a month or two could do the job to your satisfaction. Well Mr. Palm, I believe I've found myself an apartment, so now I really do need a job.

'I'm here today to make you an offer. I'll work two days for you doing any job you want to try me at. Both days are for free. If at the end of the second day you still believe I'm not your man, I'll walk out that door no questions asked. You will have had two days of free work, and I really believe I'll have proved to you that I'm the man you've been looking for.'

Jordan ran his hand through his hair, looked down at the floor and then up at the ceiling. Then leaning heavily on his right side while rubbing his chin with his right hand, he quickly looked around his shop. 'Come with me,' he said, and immediately walked to the far side of the building. Boards two feet long were stacked in several piles each approximately five feet high. Reaching he picked up a wooden box one foot long, dovetailed on all four corners. 'These boxes are for Colt pistols. Finished they'll have the words "Colt - Hartford Connecticut" stenciled on the top. The boxes will be built here at this table while using the table saw and dove-tail machine. Then they will go over to John standing near the back door. He'll affix two hinges to the top of each box and then apply the stenciling.

'We've been turning out thirty boxes a day. Colt insists we deliver fifty boxes a day beginning next month or they will cancel their contract with us. We've thirteen days to meet Colt's quota of fifty boxes. This contract alone amounts to almost fifty percent of our present business and I don't intend seeing it going elsewhere.

'So there you have it. I'm willing to give you two days to show me you can do the job. If you do we'll talk pay. And if you do, I'll see that you are paid for the two free days you are offering. I'll expect you here at eight tomorrow morning.' Having said that, Jordan turned and walked away.

Standing and stretching his arms and legs, he turned to Jessie and continued, "I stayed and watched the young man putting the boxes together. A two-foot long board was marked and cut directly at its center producing two boards each exactly one-foot long. This process was repeated using a second board from the pile. All four boards were then taken over to the dove tail machine. Another board was chosen from the top of the pile and cut in four equal parts two of which were also dove tailed after applying them to the opposite side of the dove tailing machine. The other two pieces were then set aside to be used on a later box. Turning the long pieces on end, a rubber mallet was struck securing one end piece in place. Another board was cut producing two one-foot lengths that would become the top and bottom of the finished product. Several tacks were then driven through the bottom board attaching it to both sides.

"I figured at least twenty minutes had passed in making this first box I'd observed. The young man turned toward me, smiled and then walked the finished box over to the man waiting by the door. Returning to his desk the man began the process of making a new box once again. When the second box was completed I approached the man named John who would be attaching the two hinges to the top of the box and doing the stenciling. "I take it this box is now finished and ready to be shipped to Hartford," I asked after the hinges were set in place and the stenciling was complete.

"John reached out and shook my hand, telling me that for his part it was finished. But when it arrived in Hartford, they'd lay a cloth inside that would cover the bottom with enough extra to fold over the pistol they would be putting into this box. They would also place three stops, one above the barrel and two below the gun to hold it in position. Then they'd fold the remaining cloth over the gun and tack it to the inside of the box to insure the pistol wouldn't move or get damaged when it was shipped from Colt.

"I stayed a little over one hour watching the process, then left the shop. Walking to the Lobster Kettle I took a seat on the front porch and ordered myself a beer. For over an hour I thought about all I'd observed at the woodworking shop. By the time I'd finished my glass of beer, I'd assured myself that I had a job at the shop.

"Ordering another beer and an order of clam cakes, I began thinking about pay. I'd been given no idea what Mr. Jordan Palm intended offering, but I set my mind on considering nothing less than four dollars a day. In my mind I'd already figured how we could double the box output starting the very first day. I also had some questions I wanted to ask Mr. Palm regarding the operation. The Civil War was over, as to just where Mr. Jordan Palm intend taking the business, and had he even given the question any thought, I wondered?

"The following day I arrived at the box making building promptly at eight o'clock. Walking to where the boards were stacked waiting to be cut, I took twelve down from the pile and over to the table saw. Removing the ruler and pencil from the work area, I quickly installed a stop on the end of the table so that when a board was placed against it, the cut would be made exactly centered at one foot. Within minutes I had placed each board up against the stop and made the cut. In less than two minutes all twelve boards were reduced to one foot in length.

"Turning to the dove tailing machine, I dovetailed both ends of each board I'd just cut. Six inches from the saw blade I installed a second stop. This stop caused each board I now brought to the table to be cut at six inches. Removing another twelve boards from the pile I reduced each into six inch lengths. These I dovetailed also. It was at this point that Mr. Palm arrived and stood by my side."

'Over the weekend,' Simon said, 'I would like to install a piano stool and bolt this dovetailing machine onto it. Presently I'm walking from this side to the other side to do the dovetailing on the end pieces. With the piano stool installed I can stay right here by the cutting table and rotate the stool so the end dovetails will turn to me. I've just made six boxes in under twenty minutes compared to one box I watched being made in fifteen minutes yesterday.' Simon smiled broadly at Mr. Palm. 'By my method I figure you'll turn out fifty boxes by noontime each day. It'll be up to you if you want to stop there and send the people home, or maybe work until three or four o'clock and more than double your day's production.'

Mr. Jordan Palm examined the stops Simon had put in place and thought about the idea of rotating the dovetailing machine. 'Any other thoughts you've had since yesterday?'

'Actually, yes!' Simon answered. 'The Civil War is over. I suspect Colt firearms along with possibly others will be looking to the west. Hunting will be a great source of meat for people here in the east. Then there is the Indian problem the government will be forced to deal with. Pistols and rifles will be in as great a demand as they were during our Civil War. Migration will be something to consider also. Those in the South took a real beating in the war. Many will now want to start over elsewhere. Some will come north, but I suspect many will choose to go west. I'm thinking Colt will be wanting a piece of the action those out west will be providing. It'll be a new market that very well could mean additional business for you also.'

Simon paused and stepped away from the table he'd been working at. 'First off I'd like to know if you're interested in hiring me, and if so at what price.'

'I'm thinking three dollars a day to start,' Jordan said.

'At three dollars a day the only start you'll see is me starting for the door.' Simon said. 'I'll consider four dollars a day to start only if we can agree on talking about raising my pay in let's say two months. As I told you yesterday, I believe I have an apartment I'll be paying for, and other expenses will come along now with me having this job.'

'Four dollars a day it is,' Jordan said reaching out and shaking Simon's hand. 'Tomorrow starts the weekend, so I'll expect you to begin work here on Monday.' Reaching into his pocket Jordan removed eight dollars. 'This covers the two days we talked about earlier. I suspect you put several hours of thinking into what you've shown me here at the table, along with the obvious consideration you've given to the company's future.'

Later that day Simon stopped by and talked with Matt about renting a room. Matt showed him a large bedroom at the rear of the house. A smaller room adjoining this bedroom held a closet along with a desk and chair. It also possessed a door leading outside that would provide Simon with a private entrance. 'Now I realize there are no kitchen facilities available,' Matt said. 'We'll just see how we get on with each other, and maybe we can work something out regarding this in the near future. Taking that into consideration, I'll be asking ten dollars a month for the apartment. Rent to be paid on the first of each month.'

'We're about half way through this month today,' Simon said. Taking five dollars from his wallet he handed it to Matt. 'Come the first of next month I'll be paying the full ten dollars. And my offer to help out around here still stands.'

Within the hour he was showing Darlene his new apartment. Taking the chair from the other room, he placed it at the foot of the bed. Ever so slowly he began undressing Darlene laying her clothes on the chair until she stood naked before him. 'No cane this time, and no riding crop either,' Simon said. 'Starting today we're equal. I'll not play the slave, and you will not be my master. I believe with all my heart that in time you will come to respect me as I do you.'

For three months Simon worked for Mr. Jordan Palm producing boxes that would be shipped to Colt firearms in Hartford. In 1868, Darlene gave birth to a baby boy that she and Simon named Simon Abraham Jackson. Both Simon and Darlene had decided when she knew that she was pregnant, that if it was to be a boy, they would name him Simon.

'We can't go wrong naming our son after two Presidents,' Simon said. At first Darlene was against their child carrying the name Jackson which was her maiden name. Just thinking of her father caused her to shudder. He had molested her as a child, and repeatedly abused her when she was a young single woman. But Simon being focused on the names as America's Presidents finally became acceptable to Darlene.'

"By 1870, I was itching to move. I was tired of Providence, and upset with the belief that my life was becoming stagnant. Darlene also was returning to her thoughts of moving out west. Their son was now two years old. One night I began talking to Darlene as we lay together in bed."

'It's time we move on.' he said softly. I've had my fill of making boxes, and I'm thinking you've about had it with selling dresses and such. In a month I'd like for us to be gone from Providence.'

'And just where are you thinking on going?' Darlene asked.

'That first day I saw you here in Providence, you mentioned you were thinking of possibly moving somewhere out west.' Simon said. 'I've given some thought to moving out west also in the time we've been together. Making boxes for Colt's guns has caused me to realize there will be a great demand for rifles and pistols out west both for the soldiers and civilians. Between the settlers, soldiers and Indians, along with the wild animals the people will encounter, I imagine fortunes will be made by some that are willing to take the gamble of going west.'

'I suspect a good number of Southerners will be going west also. The war may well be over, but to some, seeing a black man living with a white woman will never be acceptable,' Darlene said. 'And we've our child to consider also.'

'Well, let us both really think on it, and within a month I'd like to have us come to a decision. I'm still for going out west if that is what you really want, just as I'm also still thinking about that village in Rhode Island where I first came ashore. I've done a little looking into it, and the village is called Wickford, named after a place in England. All I know is that while I was there I felt at home. Not my home in Africa, and certainly not like when I was at Pemberton Plantation. It was a comfortable feeling I had. The people there all seemed friendly, and I can't remember one person I met who didn't smile while either nodding or saying hello as they passed me,' Simon said.

'And just what would you do if we were to go out west?' Darlene asked.

'Now there is a question that the answer would have to be worth a few hundred dollars at least,' Simon whispered while pulling Darlene tighter against him and kissing her neck. 'And, in all honesty, knowing what I'd do if we decided to go down to Wickford, would also be worth another few hundred dollars he said,' as he lowered his head and kissed her breast.

'I'm still for going out west,' Darlene said. 'I've thought

and thought on this for quite some time. As you know, I was considering going out west even before you showed up here in Providence. I know there will be southerners out west now that this war is over. 'And I know there are hostile Indians there also. Then there are the soldiers I've had to consider since I'd be alone.

'I'm telling you that some nights all these thoughts just ramble around in my head and make sleep impossible. And I'll be honest with you. Were I alone it would no doubt prove a real problem for me. Now if you were to decide to go west with me that just might even make my being there with you even worse. The Southerners we'd run into I'm sure just couldn't abide a white woman living with a black man. The Indians and the soldiers could just add to our problems.

'Yet on that first night we slept together, when you said you believed that I'd come to respect you, I didn't realize respecting you would only be a single step in our relationship. Simon, I'd come to love you long before our child was born, and that love has grown with each passing day to a point where being without you is to me just plain unthinkable now.'

Simon pushed the covers further down until they rested upon her knees. Pulling her close once again he remained silent for a few minutes while he wiped stray tears from both her and his eyes. 'I've dealt with Southerners, and believe me there are many more good ones than there are bad. I think of Blue and the other slaves at Pemberton, and a day doesn't get past me that I don't worry over them and how they are living now.

'Mr. Jonathan and even Mr. Temper were fair and honest men. They were living at a time that hopefully will never come again. Yet they both treated everyone at Pemberton fairly. Mister Temper didn't like you and didn't think much of me either. But he did his job and never back talked you, or took a whip to me.'

Simon pulled Darlene's bed covers back up and tucked them against her shoulders. 'If we do go out west, I believe we'll be able to deal with any Indians, Southerners and soldiers we come across. To possibly give us a better start, I'll talk with Mr. Richard Jarvis at Colt's when I'm in Hartford next. I've met him a few times when I've been delivering boxes. He's always taken the time to talk with me and I know he not only likes me, but is now doing business out west. Maybe he'd even consider hiring me in some small way to represent him out west with either the military or possibly the many civilians to whom he sells his guns.'

Simon smiled and said, 'Listen to me going on as if I wasn't African. Never crossed an Ocean, never saw a plantation. Hadn't walked knee deep through swamps putting all that behind me, and then helped sail a boat to New England. And as I look at the beautiful lady laying naked beside me tonight, why I suspect that the Indians,

Southerners and soldiers wouldn't give us a lick of trouble if they knew who they were dealing with.

'But just in case, the next time I'm in Hartford, I'm buying a colt pistol directly from Mr. Jarvis himself. I'll practice shooting until I'm confident I can protect us both if and when we do decide to go west. Why I just might even buy myself a rifle along with the pistol. I see no reason you can't learn to handle a pistol, then for certain sure we'd make a pair. Me with a rifle laying over my shoulder, and you having your pistol strapped to your leg in plain view for everyone to see, now there's a picture!

'The way I see it, that waitress Mary Beck that I met in New Bedford with her belaying pin in her apron, and her eight inch dagger hanging from her belt couldn't hold a candle to the picture you'd present to anyone setting eyes on you. But now before I go and fall asleep, I want to thank you for your saying how your feelings have grown for me. And little Simon means more to me than you will ever know. There is just no way I'd want to continue living if the two of you weren't in my life.'

'You know something,' Darlene said. 'I've told you I want to see the mountains out west. But more than that, I've had it with Rebels and Yankees and that foolish war. I want to see the native people out west who never experienced the Civil War. I want us to see the animals out there also, and I want our son to grow up in a different world than you and I have known. It's not just the mountains, I want us to see the trees and the rivers. I just know the world is going to be very different out west. Why I'll bet that even the air out there will be different.'

The following week, Simon arranged to take a shipment of boxes to Colt at Hartford. Within fifteen minutes of being in the building he saw Richard Jarvis approaching him. 'Mister Jarvis, May I have a minute or two of your time?' Simon asked.

'Just what can I do for you, Simon,' Richard asked as he sat down on a packing crate while directing Simon sit beside him. 'Do tell me you're thinking of leaving working in Providence and possibly considering seeking employment here at Colt.'

'That would be something I wouldn't hesitate doing. But the fact is my lady and I are considering heading out west. It has been a dream she has held ever since leaving South Carolina. We've given this several months of thought and finally decided if we are ever to do this, then now seems to be the proper time for us to actually make the move.

'My first thought is to purchase both a rifle and a pistol manufactured here at Colt. The rifle for me, the pistol for Darlene. We figure to spend a month firing these weapons and becoming familiar with them. At that time I'd give Mister Jordan Palm notice that I'll be leaving his employment. As for seeking work with Colt firearms, I'd be thrilled to work for you in the west however you may see fit to employ me.'

'Well now Simon, you've given me quite a bit to think upon. But first off before you leave here today to return to Providence, I'd like to present you with both a Colt rifle and a pistol as a personal gift. I'll also supply you with enough ammunition to insure you become both knowledgeable and proficient with these weapons.' Richard stood up and turned to face Simon. 'I do believe that in the space of a month you will have mastered both guns. By the time my man has off loaded the boxes you've brought today, I'll return with the weapons I've promised you. In a month I'll expect you back here and I'll have given serious consideration as to employing you as an agent of Colt out west.'

That night back at the apartment, Simon related to Darlene everything that had been said when he'd spoken with Richard Jarvis earlier in the day. He'd also placed a blanket on the small table they had acquired within two months of Simon first moving into this small apartment. On the blanket lay both the rifle and the pistol Richard Jarvis had given him. 'I can't say for honest sure,' Simon said. 'But I do believe Mister Jarvis will hire me when we start on our trip out west. Samuel Colt died in January of 1862. Mister Jarvis was his brother-in-law. He seems to have a good handle on the company.'

Each and every day for the following three weeks Simon

and Darlene practiced shooting with these weapons. At night they would clean both guns running small pieces of cloth down the barrel until both barrels shined as Simon held a candle up to them. On that first Friday following a week of shooting, Simon dismantled the rifle for the first time. It was late on Saturday when he finally reassembled the weapon satisfied with his effort. The following week he tackled the pistol. This went so much faster, and within three hours he'd mastered it also.

After looking at several wagons, and asking a hundred questions he finally settled on a wagon he believed to be less than one year old. Oddly enough, this wagon had been made less than four blocks from his apartment. Simon considered it a bonus in that this wagon had seldom left the shop where it had been assembled. Its only use had been delivering parts occasionally to customers. The horse used to haul it became lame three months ago and was sold to a local butcher, since that time the wagon remained in the shed beside the factory.

Adding to his relief, the price he paid for this wagon was less than the prices asked for each and every wagon he'd already looked at. Counting his remaining money once again, he began looking for a horse to buy. On the second day of his search he felt he'd found the perfect horse. Following three days of dickering with the owner over the price being asked, Simon considered he'd shaved a little over ten percent off the owner's price and bought the animal.

That evening Simon and Darlene attempted to set a date for starting west. 'I've got notice to give to Mister Palm, and we've got supplies to buy and load the wagon. I've talked with Matt off and on, and he knows we'll be leaving soon. Money is getting short, and I've been thinking that maybe I can find a small job here and there as we make our way west…just enough to keep us going, and maybe with a little extra to spare.'

'And will you be going on this trip alone?' Darlene asked smiling. 'I've still got most of the money Jonathan gave me when we divorced. Not once have you asked me about it. You bought the wagon and horse, and you've paid the rent here every month since you moved in and asked me to move in with you. If I'm to be a part of this western adventure I intend paying my share.'

'Now don't go getting all head up,' Simon said. 'I've given thought to whatever money you may have, but I've also given thought to what if anything happens to me! We're not married and I can't see anyway or anywhere we can get married. I've been a slave and I'm black. Once we begin this journey any number of things could happen to me leaving you alone with young Simon in the middle of God only knows where. You'll need money even if it's just to get you back here to Providence. I realize you can sell the horse and wagon and possibly take a train back here. But there are so many unknowns awaiting us, I just want to assure myself that you and little Simon won't suffer in any way once we start out.'

'I've a little under a thousand dollars tucked away,' Darlene said. 'I spent very little of the money Jonathan gave me, and precious little of what I've worked for and earned since I left Pemberton. As I said to you that first day, my thoughts were on eventually going somewhere out west. While I would have loved to have actually seen the mountains that I've only seen pictures of, I knew all along that being alone and the journey I'd be taking on may very well have forced me to settle somewhere in New York or even as far away from Providence as Ohio. But you have opened up a complete new world for me. Now I've you and little Simon, and even just sitting here we are sharing a dream together.

'A dream I never could have imagined alone. Already we have a horse and wagon. And we've each got a weapon were now familiar with. You alone have made all this possible. I believe I know the groceries we will need before we start out. I will purchase these with my money along with extra clothes I believe we'll be needing. Once we begin, if it becomes necessary for you to take on work to supplement our money, there is no reason I also can't find employment which will no doubt cut our down time in half. But for the moment little Simon is asleep. Kicking back the covers she whispered make love to me now.'

The next day, as Matt Johnson bounced little Simon on his knee, trying his best to keep tears from his eyes, he cleared his throat once again and began speaking to the boy's father, 'Now I've known for some time that you and your lady have been thinking on moving somewhere out west,' Matt began.

'I got to tell you Simon, you've been a good and decent friend to me ever since the day you moved in here. And Darlene is a wonder for sure. Now if there was just some way I could get you both to leave little Simon with me as you start heading west, my life would be perfect. I just know I'll miss that little boy each and every day of my life.' Matt said as he pulled a small packet out of his pocket, and handed it to Simon. 'It's not much, a month or two's rent money that just may come in handy somewhere along the way. And I decided to match that when I was putting the packet together. The extra is for Darlene and little Simon. Know that a large part of my heart will be going right along with you three as you follow your dream west. And I'll be asking you to keep in touch with me whenever you find it possible. I've no family of my own as I've told you before. So when the good Lord decides He needs me, I'll be leaving this property to you. Hell, I'll be dead and gone so it won't mean a lick to me what you decide to do with the house and grounds. I'll leave that decision in your hand.'

Chapter 5
Heading West

"Darlene, little Simon, and I left Providence about one week after talking with Matt. Darlene had that wagon filled to the top of the sideboards," Simon said. "She had clothes, blankets and sheets in there, and enough food to keep us going without having to stop for two or three weeks. I had every tool I could lay my hands on during those last couple of weeks before we started out, most in a box in the wagon, but some strapped to the outside. The rifle I kept in a leather case under the seat, while Darlene holstered her pistol high up on her leg under her skirt.

"I took two days this time getting to Hartford. Everything we passed was so new to Darlene, I just found myself pulling back on the reins and letting the horse rest a bit while Darlene soaked in the beauty of all she was seeing. And I got to tell you that, although I'd passed this way several times delivering boxes to Colt, it was on this trip with Darlene and little Simon that I really first took notice of just how pretty this country was that we were going through.

"At Hartford, I pulled right up to the loading dock at

Colt's. Ever true to his word, Richard stepped on that dock as soon as he heard I'd arrived. Within minutes he'd sent off for some food and ordered a table brought out onto the dock for the four of us to sit around. He also stepped aside and told one of his men to measure our wagon and come up with a waterproof tarp to cover everything inside. To say he took a liking right off to Darlene would be way off the mark. And little Simon ended up spending half of our time on that dock sitting on Richard's lap. When we'd finished eating, Richard asked if we'd settled upon final plans regarding our intended destination."

'To be honest with you I've an interest in seeing St. Louis,' Simon said. 'I do understand that the jumping off place for going out west is considered to be St. Joseph at the opposite side of the state. Then again, other people have told me Kansas City is the place I should be giving consideration too. I'm hearing it all depends on if we'll be planning on taking the Oregon Trail, or possibly the more southern Santa Fe Trail. Presently, I'm thinking more along the lines of the Oregon Trail. Again, Darlene wishes to see the mountains more than anything, and I suspect the Oregon Trail will fill that wish best.'

'You do realize you're in for quite a journey,' Richard said. 'I have men already out west, and I have to tell you several have been killed just within this past year. The trip west is nothing like the life we experience here.

'First off you'll have the distance to contend with. Most folks gather together and pay a guide that knows the country to assist them. If a wagon breaks down and is beyond repair, you can figure at least half of your belongings will be staying put with the wagon. That's if you can find someone in the group that has room for you in their wagon.

'And presently there is little or no law out west. The young and the strong will take whatever they want, and the closest thing to any semblance of law will be the army that well may be fifty or one hundred miles away. You'll be constantly crossing over hostile Indian land, and while in no way am I trying to discourage you, I know for a fact that you'll find many a grave marker beside the trail you're on.

'Not to be morbid but those grave markers are not always where the dead are buried. Most always a grave is dug further along at the center of the trail and then covered over. All wagons bound for the west roll over those graves. In that way the scent of the bodies buried below is hopefully removed from roaming wild animals and the dead are left to rest in peace.'

Richard paused and shifted little Simon who had fallen asleep onto a chair beside him and next to the boy's mother. 'The Indians will vary from tribe to tribe. Most as I say will be hostile, but some will be willing to trade for whatever it is they want, or think you have. Liquor is high on their list along with rifles. Many are thieves and will steal even as you are watching them.

'One man working for me saw an Indian lift a frying pan from the fire and dump out the bacon the people were cooking. He wanted that frying pan for his wife and that's all there was to it. Most times they will trade for what they covet. Often your team leader will be able to speak the Indian's language. If so, he'll advise you that liquor and guns are not to be traded regardless of what is offered or how apparently dangerous the situation becomes.' Richard shifted in his seat before he spoke once again.

'Seems to me, that times are changing at a rapid pace,' Richard said. 'The west is a whole different story from how the east was settled. Back in 1831, before the Civil War the Government saw fit to move the Indians in the southeastern part of this country to the land west of the Mississippi. Now it wasn't pretty, and I believe most white people would be liking to forget all about it. In eighteen and thirty-one, the Choctaw were shuffled off to land designated as Indian Territory west of the Mississippi. Well once the precedent was set, the Government moved the Creek, then the Chickasaw in 'thirty-seven, and the Cherokee in 'thirty-eight.

'It's known as the trail of tears. Those Indians were forced from their homes and some thirteen thousand Native American Indians lost their lives due to prolonged exposure, disease and starvation during that relocation. But the result according to the Government was that twenty-five million acres were then opened for white settlement. I'm thinking the Indians out west will be digging their heels in so as to not allow a repeat of that tragedy.

'It has not been my intention to dissuade you from going west,' he continued, 'I have learned much from those working for me in the west and this I want to pass along to you. Some good things you should know. If at all possible, pick a group that includes a doctor. There will be enough women-folk along to assist with birthing babies and such. But a doctor can be the difference between life and death for those traveling on your journey. I already have planned to supply you with pistols, possibly as many as fifty to start. These I'll have waiting for you in St. Louis. I would also advise you to invest in a moderate amount of liquor before you start out from here. Not for the Indian trade, but as gifts for those traveling with you and soldiers you will no doubt encounter. Then again, you'll find that liquor can be a godsend in many a medical situation.'

'Darlene and I both want to see the mountains further out west, so St. Louis is a place I have in my mind where we can catch a breather, possibly work a little, and raise some additional income if necessary before we make the plunge west. I'm also of the belief from everything I've heard that St. Joseph will be the end of the line for our wagon. Everyone I've talked with tells me that I'll be needing a covered wagon if we're to continue west. And from what I'm hearing we'll possibly be replacing the horse with a team of oxen at that time also. Now all this information is new to me, and I can't say as it's all true. I do suspect a covered wagon, which I'm told are called Conestoga wagons, carry at least five times the amount of goods that the wagon we have now is capable of carrying.' Simon said.

'I thank you for all the information you shared with us,' Darleen said. 'Simon and I will never forget the many kindnesses you gave to us and our son. I have one favor to request. I would consider it a great treasure if you would consider yourself Little Simon's Godfather. We would rest easier knowing that our son would have some "family" he could count on if we died on the trail.' Darlene squeezed Simon's hand and watched Richard for his reaction and with tears of joy asked, 'Can I take it that your nod and tears means you will do that for us?'

"Our family left Hartford headed west that afternoon and camped among a grove of evergreen trees after covering about seven miles. We stopped again for the night at Preston, Connecticut and arrived at Bulls Bridge late the following evening. The next morning we crossed over into New York by ferry.

"It was shortly after leaving the ferry that we encounter our first incident of racial intolerance. Two scruffy looking men were walking along the roadside in the same direction as we were going. One had on a worn pair of grey pants with a yellow stripe down the side of each leg, beyond a doubt an ex-Confederate. He stood almost six feet tall and wore a straw hat covering long brown hair that poked out from below his hat and rested upon his shoulders. His companion was much shorter, and his clothes were a collection he'd gathered since leaving the South. Neither his shirt nor pants actually did fit him, and he, unlike his tall friend, was walking barefoot.

'Hold up there!' the tall man said as he grabbed hold of the bridle on the horse. 'Woman, why don't you order your Nigger down from that wagon and let us two men ride and rest our feet awhile?'

'I'll be asking you kindly,' Darlene spoke softly, 'to let go of the horse's bridle, and step back away from our wagon.'

'Well, Hell lady, I can tell from your talking that you're a born southerner.' The tall man spoke again while still holding the horse's bridle. 'You should know better than to back a Black over two white men who served along-side Master Robert himself.'

'The war is over, and the Confederacy, along with slavery, no longer exists in this country,' Darlene said. 'I'll ask you for the last time to let loose of the horse's bridle.'

'You know my temper is getting short,' the man said in a loud, demanding way, 'and I'm thinking of dragging you both off that wagon."

Darlene calmly withdrew her pistol and aimed it at the man's head. 'If your hand isn't off that bridle in ten seconds you'll be laying in the road a dead man. Now I want you and your friend to step off the side of the road and sit yourselves down until we are completely out of sight.'

'I don't take kindly to a woman pointing a pistol at me and threatening to shoot me,' the man said as he let loose of the horse's bridle and stepped back beside his friend standing at the edge of the road. 'I've a good memory, and I'll not be forgetting you or your Nigger any time soon.'

'If I were you, I'd thank my lucky stars that I alone handled this situation and didn't involve my companion. As for not forgetting either of us, that sir would be the height of foolishness for you. For me this unfortunate incident is over and done with.' Saying this, Darlene nodded to Simon, and with a flick of his wrist he gently settled the reins on the horse's back and their wagon rolled forward.

Two days later they crossed Dingman's Ferry taking them into Pennsylvania and made their way to Tobyhanna before stopping for the night. 'I don't see much of a need for us going any further,' Simon said while smiling at Darlene. 'Mostly all you've talked about is seeing the mountains out west. Well just you look around us, we're surrounded by mountains higher than anything I've ever seen.

'I haven't a clue how we'll thread our wagon through these mountains and manage to come out still headed west. Why just today we've passed at least six beautiful waterfalls, and most every one of these mountains appear to reach half way up to the clouds.

'This has to be the most beautiful country I have ever set my eyes on. Everything is so lush and green. Just you look where we are right now. Africa where I lived has nothing like this that I ever saw. South Carolina can't begin to compare, and some of the places I've been since landing in Rhode Island while they are very nice and were what I'd call welcoming, they still can't hold a candle to right where we're standing.'

Darlene paused before speaking and slowly turned in a full circle taking in everything in sight. Turning back to Simon she said, 'All I know of the west is from the paintings I've seen. While I'll admit this is beautiful country, I for one am all for pushing on with our original plan. If we find the west to be less than what I've dreamed it to be, we can always come back here. But we'll never know until we continue on.'

Two evenings later they camped in Berwick. Another day's travel brought them to Milton at the foot of the Appalachian Mountains of Pennsylvania. 'If, and when, we cross over these mountains, we'll be in Ohio if I've been told the truth.' Simon shaded his eyes and looked at the mountains standing tall before them. 'My choice is to camp right here for a few days. I've seen at least twelve deer today during our journey, so I feel pretty sure I can hunt us up some fresh meat without breaking much of a sweat.

'And there is a large lake right over there,' he said pointing. 'That tells me we've drinking water and possibly some fresh fish available to us also. There's plenty of good grass for the horse. Plus stopping here for a couple of days will give us the chance to square away our gear and straighten up the inside of our wagon.'

Simon playfully smacked Darlene on her backside while saying, 'Little Simon's sleeping. When he wakes up we'll be sure to give him a good bath also. Meanwhile, last one in the lake is going to be the last one to feel clean all over again since we left New York.' With that said, Simon peeled off his clothes as he ran toward the water. Within a minute Darlene dove in naked beside him.

Simon, Darlene and their son stayed four days beside the lake in Pennsylvania. Just at dusk following their swim, Simon shot a Buck deer as it came down toward the lake. Gathering stones, Simon built a fire pit. There was enough dry downed wood within walking distance of their wagon that fire was never a problem throughout their stay. Venison steaks and chops were cooked that first night, meanwhile Darlene cut several long strips of meat that she hung over a tree branch close to the wagon. 'I'd give anything for a block of ice or maybe even an extra tub of salt so we wouldn't have to use what's left of our original supply to preserve some of this meat,' Darlene lamented.

"Nine weeks later we finally arrived in St. Louis. 1865-1900 would in later years be referred to as 'The Golden Age of St. Louis.' It was August 7th 1871 when I turned our wagon onto 4th street. This was the business area of St. Louis. It consisted of hotels, office buildings, banks and general stores. The Hotel Southern stood at the corner of 4th and Walnut Street. It had opened in 1865 within a month of the Civil War ending.

"Immediately following the war, St. Louis boomed. By 1870 the population stood at 310,869. It was the 4th largest city in America. Horse car tracks were begun in 1859 on Olive St, then on 4th and 10th. This afforded those riding the horse-drawn trolley a smoother ride than originally traveling over rough cut stones that made up the original roadway. Throughout the city French and Spanish heritage still prevailed in the architecture. The main street was originally called the King's Highway, then changed to Rue de Royal by the French, and Camino Royal by the Spanish. Camp Jackson was captured by Union Troops in August of 1861 and held by the North throughout the war. By 1870 St. Louis became a terminus for starting west on the Santa Fe Trail."

'Checking at the Hotel Southern, Simon learned that Colt firearms had forwarded a box to him containing fifty Colt revolvers. Checking them later, he smiled seeing each revolver was in a box made and stenciled at Mr. Jordan Palm's small factory in Providence, Rhode Island.

'Got this box for you one week ago today,' Tom Dupuis said. 'I'm the manager here at the Southern. Many days I'm here at least five or six hours each day and that includes Saturdays and Sundays. Seeing the address was from Colt in Hartford, I locked it in my private office. It took two men to manhandle it, so I'll be having one of my boys give you a hand getting it out to your wagon. Will you be staying in St. Louis long?' he asked.

'I won't have an answer to that question for at least another day or two.' Simon said. 'First off I've got to find a place to stay. I hope I can rent a small place in or close to the city. Then I'll be deciding if I need to find employment for a short while before I again head west with my family. But what I've seen today has taken my breath away. We were in Providence for a while, and then started this trip west from Hartford. But my Lord! Trolleys running down the middle of Main Street, and buildings such as I've never seen before.' Simon shook his head, then looked at the interior of this hotel before he spoke again. 'I've spent time in Rhode Island and as I've said we started this journey at Hartford, nowhere else have I seen buildings like I'm seeing here in St. Louis.'

Tom smiled and said, 'There is a lot of holdover from the French and Spanish who were here long before this present population arrived. Now I'm from Canada myself. I was an assistant manager of a small hotel in Montreal for two years, until the owners learned that the manager was using hotel money for his own purposes. They fired him and moved me up as manager. That lasted a little over a year when they asked me to come down to St. Louis, and have a look at this new hotel they were building. Taking everything into consideration, I still believe I made the right choice staying here." Tom smiled and knocked on the wooden countertop.

'The Civil War ended one month before we opened our door here at the Southern. I had serious hotel competition right here on 4th Street and over on Market Street, but I saw to it every day and in every way that the Southern would always be the first choice of travelers. I hired a young girl whose only job was gathering fresh cut flowers. We put these beautiful flowers in each and every room and changed them out every two days. We were also the only hotel that provided free tea and pastry for our guests every day in our foyer from four until five o'clock in the afternoon. When I learned of a birthday or anniversary, I substituted the tea for a glass of wine for that person. These might have all just been little things, but the word spread and seldom are we not fully booked.'

'Well with these arches and carriage lamps, along with the beautiful inlays in these pillars reaching from floor to ceiling, I feel like I'm standing in another world,' Simon observed. 'It's certainly a world I've never known before. And in my lifetime, I've never seen the likes of these rugs covering the floor. I can't even imagine what your rooms must look like.'

'Well when you have the time, stop in and I'll give you a personal tour of the hotel. Meanwhile, I do know of a small house that I believe is available to rent about five blocks from here.' Tom called over a girl dusting the banister. 'Do you know if the James house is still vacant?' he asked.

'Since Mr. James died, Martin has been keeping watch over there off and on when he's not working the night shift here at the hotel. I'm sure there is nobody living there, but Martin will know for certain sure,' the girl said.

'Martin is out back staining a railing,' Tom said. 'Come along with me and we'll both learn the answer at the same time.' Martin was a short man who didn't appear to have a neck. His head looked like it sat right on his shoulders. He was slightly darker of skin tone than Simon. Later Simon learned Martin had escaped from a Louisiana plantation early in 1862 and been caught within two weeks by Hawkers, and returned to his owner's plantation. Today he was staining a railing that ran the length of the back porch.

'Now don't you be touching this railing, or even letting your clothes get up against it.' Martin said. 'It'll take a good month before you get this stain off your hand. And as for your clothes, Hell, you might just as well burn them or throw them away, because you'll never get them clean again no matter what you do. Mr. Dupuis, I'll be putting a rope all around this railing along with a couple of boards blocking guests from getting anywhere near it before it has had time to dry.'

'Thank you Martin, but I'll be bolting the back door whenever you tell me you're finished for the day.' Tom said. 'What we're here for is to learn if the James house is vacant. Mr. Simon here is looking for a place to hold up for a week, maybe a month or two. He and his family are headed west.'

'Right now there is no one there. I'm the only one who checks the house out a couple of times a week. It sure would be good to have someone living there even if it was just for a short while until it's sold. I'd like to get a dollar a day out of whoever stays there.' Martin said. 'Give me fifteen minutes to clean up what I'm doing here, and I'll take you out the James place myself, if that's alright with Mr. Dupuis.'

One hour later Martin was showing Simon and Darlene the James house. Taking Simon aside he said, 'I know I said I wanted a dollar a day from whoever rents this place, but between you and me fifty cents a day is all I want from you. Mr. Dupuis will no doubt set the rent amount, but I suspect you and I have walked somewhat the same road that's brought us both to this point.

'When the war ended I was given forty acres of land at the plantation I was at. I also was given a mule. This was all a government program, so I guess I should have known that those in Washington would sooner or later go back on their word. Sure enough just about the time my first crop was coming in, the government ordered the land given back to the plantation owner. This owner was the same useless cruel being that had taken a whip to both my wife and daughter after he'd stripped them both naked and tied them to the fence.

'Well he told me my mule was only worth fifty cents. Throwing the money for the mule on the ground at my feet he told me to get off his property. Yes, I guess I can say that not much has changed for our people since the war ended. And that fifty cents, as far as I know, is still laying in the dirt where he threw it. I took my wife and daughter north with me and promised myself that I'd never step on Southern soil again as long as I lived.

'Now we get ex-confederates in here all the time. I surely do enjoy ignoring them every chance I get. I can see the hatred in their eyes when I ignore them, but they can't see me smiling on the inside. Mr. Dupuis doesn't take any truck from them either. Many a time when they have made a complaint against me, Mr. Dupuis tells them that he believes they might just be more comfortable at another hotel.'

'To be honest with you, I'm more interested and concerned

with having the security of the house with you and your family being there than anything else,' Tom said. 'So five dollars a week is satisfactory with me. By the way, another box arrived from Colt in Hartford for you, it came in yesterday. Both are in my office.' The second box held two hundred rounds of ammunition for the Colt pistols.

'I thank you for the generous offer on the rent, and yes, we'll move in as soon as you say we can,' Simon said while reaching out and shaking Tom's hand. After settling in the house, it took two full days for Simon and Darlene to figure out their finances, along with their needs for continuing west. Money-wise they were comfortable with how much money they still had on hand.

'We'll be needing to restock the wagon with food before we move on,' Darlene said, 'and from what I've learned, prices are a little higher here than they were back in Providence, or what we've been paying along this trip so far. I'd suggest you check and see if you couldn't sell five or six pistols right here in St. Louis at let's say fifteen or even twenty-five dollars each. I have no idea what the going price of a new Colt pistol is. That is something you'll have to find out yourself.'

The next day, Simon walked into Bob Banville's general store. 'I'm interested in what you have in the way of a decent pistol,' Simon asked.

Bob walked Simon down to a counter located midway in

the shop. 'Mostly people are buying rifles,' Bob said. 'Then again, I'd guess eighteen out of every nineteen rifles I sell are bought by people headed west. Remington seems to me to be the most requested rifle along with Winchester.

'I do sell several different makes of pistols, but Colt holds the lead among the various ones I carry. I'm a little short on Colt revolvers right now, but I do happen to have one new Colt, along with two used models I've taken in recently. The new Colt I can let you have for twenty-dollars. I'm looking to get possibly fifteen dollars out of one of the used ones and ten out of the other. Mind you, both of the used pistols are good. But they are used, and while both have signs of wear on them, one also really does need a new set of grips.'

'Well I'll be representing Colt once I get myself out west. Meanwhile, Richard Jarvis of Colt Firearms; has already sent me a shipment of his newest revolver. These are mint in the box revolvers. I'd be willing to part with six of them if we could come to an agreeable price,' Simon said as he handed the store owner a letter of introduction from Colt Firearms. Simon walked outside and reached under the seat of his wagon. Taking one Colt box from under the blanket he'd covered it with, he returned to the store. 'Now for a little history, I made some of these boxes when I worked in Providence, Rhode Island. I delivered finished boxes to Colt firearms at Hartford. That is how our relationship developed. I'd be willing to sell you six exactly like this one for twenty-five dollars each.

Bob Banville carefully opened the box and looked at the new revolver. 'There isn't much profit for me at twenty-five dollars each, but they are beautiful, and I'll possibly make some extra money selling a holster to whoever buys one. Any chance,' Bob asked, 'you would consider fifteen-dollars each for six?'

'You know my family and I left Hartford after having lunch with Richard Jarvis at Colt. Hartford is many miles from St. Louis, and going west we've got possibly as far, if not further, travel laying ahead of us to be crossed. As you say, you'll make a profit no matter if you raise your price, or just sell a holster, or maybe even some ammunition when you sell the pistol.' Simon stopped talking and thought for a short while. 'Bob, I'll be holding to my asking twenty-five dollars each for the six identical pistols I'll be selling you.'

Bob Banville reached over the counter and shook Simon's hand. 'Twenty-five dollars it is, and God's truth, I'm pleased to get them. When will you deliver them?' Bob asked.

'If you'll have the money available in cash tomorrow afternoon, I'll be here with the six pistols.' Simon said. The following day Simon delivered the six pistols to Banville's shop and was paid cash closing the deal.

That night Simon and Darlene counted their money on hand and decided they would stay in St. Louis two, possibly four weeks. First off the three of them needed a rest, then Simon really wanted to see everything possible in the city and money didn't appear to be a problem. The following day Darlene got a job filling in for a waitress at a small restaurant right off 4th Street. The girl she replaced would only be out for two weeks, three at the most. Simon also figured just before they left, he'd try to sell Banville another six pistols. Tom was true to his word and gave Simon a complete tour of the hotel. And he insisted they all three stop by the hotel at four in the afternoon on Friday, and be his guests as refreshments were made available.

'I can't thank you enough for the feeling of security I've had regarding the James house knowing you and your family were staying there. Late last week I finally sold that property. The new owners are locals and they will be moving in the weekend after you leave. On Friday I'll see to it that you and your lady enjoy some choice wine we have here at the hotel. I understand you sold Banville some spanking new Colt revolvers. Before you leave us, I'd like to buy one from you myself.'

'I'll bring it with me the Friday before we leave. It's a gift for all you've done for me.' Simon said.

'That won't happen,' Tom said. 'I know for a fact that Bob paid twenty-five dollars for each pistol he bought from you, and I'm more than willing to do the same.'

'Well we'll avoid an argument right here and now, and I'll take a ten-dollar gold piece from you for the pistol and not a dollar more,' Simon said. 'By the way, how did you find out what Bob paid?'

'St. Louis may be a big city,' Tom said. 'But here along 4th street not much is kept secret for long. Bob was actually thrilled with his purchase. I doubt he told more than a couple of people what he paid, if that. But being as he also happens to be my brother-in-law, well you can see how it is.'

"Three weeks later, the three of us were a mile west of St. Louis before the sun broke through the morning clouds. The day before we left, I sold Bob Banville three more pistols. I gave the money for the nine pistols Bob Banville had bought to Tom, and asked him to forward it to Richard Jarvis at Colt Firearms in Hartford, Connecticut along with a short letter I had Darlene write for me. After writing the letter to Richard, Darlene wrote a letter to Matt Johnson, telling him of our travels and arrival here at St. Louis. This letter Tom also forwarded to the address in Providence, Rhode Island that I gave him.

"Little Simon was now going on three years old, and when not napping, insisted on sitting up front in the wagon between his mother and me. It took us six weeks to reach Kansas City. It was now early October, and Darlene worried about continuing on based upon the lateness of the season. After giving the situation serious consideration, we chose to push on at least to Abilene, Kansas.

RICHARD BRIAN CLARK

"It was just outside of Abilene we saw our first herd of wild Buffalo. Here the land was very flat and covered with grass as far as the eye could see. It was here also where we came upon the first troop of Army Cavalry. It was a black company referred to as 'Buffalo Soldiers', operating at half strength, with one white officer."

'You're in dangerous territory,' the Sergeant said, as he reined his mount to a halt beside their wagon. 'This is Ottawa and Chippewa hunting country. To the Ottawa those Buffalo are like pollen to a bee. I'm really surprised we're not seeing any Ottawa here now. I suspect you're headed into Abilene, am I correct?'

'We're headed west,' Simon said, 'but I do plan on holding up in Abilene possibly until spring. My lady and I haven't made a final decision just yet, but our goal is to eventually get on the Oregon Trail and continue west. She is bound and determined to see the Rocky Mountains. I'll be representing Colt Firearms once we decide to settle down.'

'Well, me and my boys will just ride along with you and see that you actually get to Abilene without having any problems. We're past due for a break anyway,' the sergeant said. 'You don't know it, but I suspect Abilene is like nothing you've ever experienced before. Mostly it's just three or four saloons, and a way station for coaches going further west or back toward St. Louis. You'll find a dozen, or maybe a few more, families who have built their homes just outside of the town. The town itself is little more than a dirt road with false front buildings on either side.

'A blacksmith shop, a drug store and only one hotel may be worth considering. And it's anything but peaceful. There will be a gun fight at least once a week that you can count on. And as far as law is concerned, you can forget about that. Cattlemen rule the roost in Abilene, and they don't take kindly to sod busters or strangers.

'With people like you just passing through, you'll do well to keep a tight grip on any money you happen to have. And I wouldn't let on that you have anything to do with Colt. When you get into Abilene you'll find yourself in the middle of nowhere, that's for certain sure. The only good thing I can say about the town is that it will eventually change for the better. Talk has it that the army may build a post there sometime. Then again, I'm hearing the circuit judge is thinking of settling there and making it his base of operation. My advice, although you're not asking me, is that you consider continuing on to Fort Lincoln, Kansas.

'It's a little out of your way, but much safer, and you'll no doubt find other settlers holding up there for the winter also. I'd be giving that option some serious thought as we make our way into Abilene.' With this said, the Sergeant nodded to Darlene and the baby, then turned and rejoined his men.

Pushing back my chair, I stood and faced Jessie, "I expect your ears must be about as tired as my mind is, listening to all I've been jawing about!" Looking out the window, I was surprised at how late in the afternoon it was!

"I'm enjoying every word you've spoken, but now, since you mention it, I am partial to taking a break," Jessie stretched as she suggested, "how about if we continue first thing in the morning?"

"Well now, Miss Jessie, your first thing in the morning might not be what I consider my first thing!" teased Simon as a broad smile spread across his face. "Why don't we say sometime around nine in the morning? I'll sit myself back down in this chair and, hopefully, we can wrap this tale up to your satisfaction then."

Jessie gathered up the loose papers she'd been keeping notes on, and setting them aside on her desk, stood and walked around the desk to shake Simon's hand and laughed,. "Tomorrow at nine, it is!"

Walking down to his gun store, Simon was reflecting on all he had said to the reporter today. 'Simon!' a man across the street hollered while waving his hat so Simon would see him.

Hurrying across the dirt street and stepping up onto the wooden walkway, the man stopped and stood facing Simon, 'Randal Peabody's my name, and I've only been in town a little over a week. I'm looking to homestead on a piece of land west of the train depot that I've put a claim in on. I'm looking to buy a rifle, along with a pistol or two. Word has it that you're the man I should be talking with.'

'My shop is only a little ways down,' Simon said pointing along the sidewalk. 'I was going there when I heard you holler. Come long and we'll see if I can't set you up with something that will suit your fancy.'

Later, when Simon locked the door to his gun shop, he was pleased with the three guns he had sold, along with the three boxes of ammunition as well. This was the first time that he raised the price on his Colt pistols to forty dollars each. Randal Peabody hadn't questioned his asking price. In less than an hour of meeting this man in the street, Simon was on his way home.

Chapter 6
Ruffled Feathers
at Fort Lincoln, Kansas

At nine the following morning, I arrived at the Lexington News office as agreed upon. "Good morning, Miss Jessie. I made some hush puppies for us to have with our morning coffee." I placed the bag of freshly made hush puppies on her desk as I sat down facing the reporter once again.

"From here on out, what I'm going to be telling you might be a bit upsetting I've given considerable thought as to what I'll be saying today, and I hope I won't be offending you. There will be some killing and some hanging. I will also be mentioning some names, and the last thing I want is to give anyone grief.

"I don't give a hoot about the Indians I'll be talking about and as to Custer, I'll be making myself plain and if anyone disagrees with what I say regarding him, well, for all I care they can just go straight to Hell! So now I've said my piece and if you're comfortable and willing, I'll be picking up where we left off yesterday.

"After discussing our options, Darlene and 1 decided to take the Sergeant's advice and make Fort Lincoln our destination for the coming winter. Shortly after telling the Sergeant of our decision, we all turned northwest toward Fort Lincoln, arriving there a day and a half later. The Fort was little more than a wooden stockade with block houses set high on the walls at each corner. Barracks, within the fort, held approximately two hundred soldiers.

"Outside the walls were camped at least three hundred Indians separated a decent distance from settlers that were headed west. Among the Indian encampment stood possibly forty teepees. Many of the Indians just built shelters and covered them with evergreen branches. When winter arrived many of these Indians would relocate to villages elsewhere, dropping the Indian population here at the fort to about one hundred, mostly woman and children. Within that first day, Darlene and I realized there were thirty families at the fort that would be starting west at the first signs of spring. Neither Indians nor civilians were allowed within the walls of the fort. The one standing exception was that every Thursday the fort's gates were guarded, but opened only to the settlers so they could take advantage of the Sutter's wares. I made it a point to acquaint himself with the Sutter along with the commanding officer at his first opportunity."

'Well bless my soul, I don't believe my eyes,' Martha said when she first spotted Simon standing beside his wagon. Running forward she threw her arms around him. 'I'd given you up for dead within two months after you ran away from Pemberton Plantation. My man and I stayed on at Pemberton following the war, and were given forty acres there to be working the land for ourselves. Master Johnathan made tools available to us, and Mr. Temper hitched up a plow to a horse, and actually helped turn the soil with us until the government finally came through with the mule they'd promised us.

'This lasted a little over a year, then the folks in Washington decided to return the whole plantation back to the original owner. Mr. Jonathan offered to pay us to stay at Pemberton and continue to work the land. He even offered to pay us for our labor. But our not having the land ourselves, some of us decided to move on. We took Shari under our wing and brought her along with us, intending to find us some land out west.'

About this time Darlene and young Simon came around from the other side of their wagon. She and Martha just stared at each other for several seconds. The tension was broken when little Simon ran toward Martha. 'I'm sure you've a whale of a story to tell James and me,' Martha said looking straight at Darlene.

'Why don't we plan on eating together tonight?' Darlene asked Martha. 'Simon killed a deer recently, and we've plenty of coffee also. It'll give us a chance to come to terms with each other. I suspect we could spend a complete night bringing each other up to date on our recent past.'

'I'll talk with James and see if he's agreeable, if so we'll join you for dinner. I'll also be bringing Shari along with us. I'm known to make an outstanding apple cobbler, so I'll be bringing that along also.' Martha turned to face Simon and said, 'I still can't believe that you are here, alive and well. I thank the good Lord for that.' Turning she walked away whispering so only she could hear, 'as for the rest we'll just have to wait and see.'

'I've heard the saying about the cow jumping over the moon,' Darlene said smiling at Simon after Martha had left. 'But I believe my settling up with Martha will be a bit more of a challenge than that cow encountered, to put it mildly.'

'You'll do just fine,' Simon said. 'God! But I can hardly wait to possibly hear about Blue and if he's alive! But Pemberton and slavery is all behind us now, as is the Confederacy. We're all here in Kansas and headed west.

'I see no reason at all to truck baggage from our past along with us as we move on. There is no way on earth we can change the past, but I'm all for burying it right here, and letting it lay.' Putting his arms around Darlene he pulled her tight against him. 'If there be a moon out tonight, we'll all just forget about jumping it and just slither under it and enjoy a good time together.'

The evening went better than anyone sitting around that rock-enclosed cooking fire anticipated. Martha could see the change in Darlene right off. Simon and Darlene talked about unexpectedly meeting up in Providence, Rhode Island. Simon told how he'd sailed North landing along the coast of Rhode Island. Darlene related how she'd made her way from Savannah up to Maryland and later to Providence, where she found work at a ladies dress shop.

Martha asserted, 'If it wasn't for the Yankee soldiers, I doubt we would have gotten as far north as Illinois.' She continued, 'Whenever the soldiers were not around, stragglers would accost us and take whatever they wanted.

'We didn't have no gun with us,' she said, 'and only when James confronted one of the thieves with a pitchfork did we manage to not have anything stolen. Why early on, one ex-Confederate actually stole two of James' shirts and a pair of his britches. Took these right out of the wagon we were pulling and laughed as he walked away. Soldiers caught up with him within the hour and got the stolen clothes back to us. Lucky for the thief, we never saw him again. James kept a hammer in his hand most of the time from that day on. I've no doubt he'd have used it if anyone tried to steal from us again.'

'What can you tell me about Blue?' Simon asked.

'Now I'll be telling you the honest truth,' James said. 'Blue, he up and had his cabin moved to the far corner of the plantation. I'm guessing somewhere close to where you must have left. He marked off about two acres while Master Jonathan and Mr. James Temper stood right there watching him. He set a pile of stone right behind his house that he'd hauled up from the creek.'

'Master Jonathan', Blue said, 'I don't care what them up in Washington come up with. I figure if it's all right with you, I'll live right here and farm these two acres for myself. When I die I'd be beholding to you to bury me right behind my cabin. You can use these rocks to cover my grave, and I'll be knowing that I'll be a free-man resting in God's forgiving peace.'

'Far as I know Blue is still there at Pemberton farming his two acres. Master Jonathan promised it would be all done as Blue had asked.'

Martha clapped her hands and smiled. 'Master Jonathan provided Blue with all the seed he needed, along with offering him free use of anything in the barn or blacksmith shop. I swear Blue is right there today with not a worry in the world bothering him.'

'And, what about Jonathan?' Darlene asked. 'But before you go to telling me about him, I just want you to know, I blame myself for all that happened between Jonathan and me. There was another man I believed I was in love with before I married Jonathan. Looking back now, I can't believe I treated Jonathan and the people at Pemberton as poorly as I did. Before I met Simon in Rhode Island, if I thought I could have gone back and been a good wife with Jonathan, I just might have tried. But events have a way of changing, and when I finally saw Simon in Providence I didn't know it at the time, but together we'd started on a complete new journey.'

'Well I guess about half the folk at Pemberton stayed on there. At first they figured they were working the land for themselves and eventually would own it. But that was not to be the case.' James said. 'I'd say a dozen or more left the plantation right off looking for a better life as free people. But that was not to be either. Within six months over half of them that left came back. Today I suppose most everyone is back working at the plantation. Now they are getting paid for their labor, but after buying clothes and other items they need from the new building Master Jonathan built and stocked as a plantation store, they're not really much better off than before the war began. I honestly don't see their lot ever improving. Maybe in some places such as Pemberton they won't be treated as slaves, but they will always be held down under the white man's boot.

'I suspect even the blacks that fought in the Union Army will now find themselves far from equal with the white soldiers they served with. I do believe that we blacks will always be a rung or two lower on the ladder than the whites. Looking around, I feel we're considered about equal with the native Indians. Hell, in some cases I guess the Indian is actually thought of more highly than us blacks.

'I'm thinking if the whites go to fighting with the Indians as we all push west, and I do believe this will be the case, then for a while those blacks in uniform serving in the army will be patted on the back, and possibly even made a fuss over. But I suspect this will pass also. No, I don't see a change coming in our lifetime, or even in any time that's to come.' James shook his head, extended his hand to Simon and Darleen, and headed to his wagon for the night.

"Two days later, I heard a scout named Roger Hawkins would be leading a wagon train west over the Oregon Trail come spring. Word had it among the settlers that this would be Hawkins' fifth crossing, and he intended taking people all the way to La Grande, Oregon. Hawkins let it be known that he considered twenty wagons was the most he'd consider guiding. He'd set his price at twenty dollars a wagon, paid in advance before he'd move a foot from Fort Lincoln.

"He also made it clear his price was strictly based on the number of wagons, and not the number of settlers. 'I don't give a hoot in Hell if a family of six or seven are traveling in their wagon. Should four or five find themselves walking instead of riding in their wagon, so be it. Some can walk all the way to Oregon for all I care. That'll be their choice. Then again, once they get to know each other they might just shift their loads to give a helping hand to one another now and then.'

Simon was up early Thursday morning and around nine o' clock he passed through the fort's gates. His first stop was to meet and introduce himself to the Sutter at the small store set against the rear wall of the fort. Mark Hopkins was a rotund man that Simon guessed would go close to four hundred pounds. Standing just a little under six feet tall, Mark wore a combination of civilian and military clothing.

Using two canes for support, he came around the counter and shook Simon's hand, 'Word here in the fort has it you represent Colt.' Mark paused waiting for some sign from Simon. 'Last night Captain Williams stopped by to ask me if I'd met you, or knew anything about you.'

Mark then began a fit of coughing and dropped one of his canes as he reached out and grasp hold of the counter. Finally catching his breath he said, 'These damn lungs of mine are about shot through and through. Then again all this extra blubber I'm carrying isn't helping me any either. We've a short spell before people begin walking in here. Why don't we both have a sit down and take a load off our legs!'

Simon reached down and picked up the cane Mark had dropped, then watched him walk around back behind the counter and take a seat. Indicating a stool at the end of the counter Mark asked Simon to pull it behind the counter closer to him, and then they could talk freely without fear of being heard.

'Captain Williams is a right good feller,' Martin began speaking. 'Fought at Gettysburg under Meade, and again with Sherman, both on his march on Savannah, and again at Bentonville in North Carolina. Several soldiers who fought alongside him said he was a real piss cutter. Didn't know the meaning of the words quit or surrender. Out here he doesn't spend any time looking over his shoulder either. Orders he gets from Washington are the law, period the end. He may not like or agree with them, but he's West Point taught, and so that's the end of it.

'Now getting to you,' Mark said pointing directly at Simon. 'Soldiers, settlers, blacks and whites, Yankees and Rebels along with Indians of several different tribes, we've a cauldron brewing here for sure. Lots of people are wanting to go west and settle on a piece of land they can call their own. But the fly in the ointment is these Indians. Most have got their heels dug in so tight that they'll never be moved off their land.

'Washington sends a hundred or two hundred soldiers out to forts here and they're thinking that will solve the problem. Well those of us already out here know them bright fellows holding power back in Washington, could send the whole US army's kit and caboodle out here, and sure as shooting, there will be a war that will eventually wake them up and make them realize what they are doing now doesn't amount to a Tinkers Damn. I have to believe that eventually the Indians will be forced onto reservations. But that will take years, not months as some folks think. And there will be an ocean of blood shed before we're done with the Indian problem.

'And I haven't begun to mention our American settlers already in Texas having broken that land away from Mexico and wanting to become part of America. My guess is this is the perfect time for a man like you to be out here representing the Colt Firearms company. But I have to tell you, I've met three men working for Winchester in the past year and a half, and all three are dead now. Indians scalped two of them, and the other got into a fight just outside this fort and bit off more than he could chew.

'As far as I know, the man that shot him hightailed it back east as fast as his horse could carry him. Captain Williams never got the chance to grab onto the man that did the killing, the law other than for Captain Williams isn't very established around here just yet.'

'I'd like to meet Captain Williams,' Simon said. 'I really don't have a clue as to how far west my family will be going. My lady Darlene wants to see the Rocky Mountains. Little Simon, our son, is just going on three years old. Richard Jarvis who is running Colt now has supplied me with a number of his newest Colt Revolvers. I received a hefty number when we stopped in St. Louis, and I suspect once I advise him we'll be holding up here for the winter I'll be seeing another shipment. I'll only be dealing with pistols. Richard figures Winchester and Remington have the rifle business out here pretty much tied up.'

Just then the door opened and a Sergeant entered,

closing the door behind him. Turning to face Simon he said, 'Captain Williams requests you stop by his office. I'm to escort you there now.'

'After you've been ridden hard by Captain Williams,' Mark said chuckling softly,' I hope you'll find your way back here and we can talk some more. Possibly even do a little business together.'

Captain Robert Williams appeared to Simon to be somewhere in his late twenties. Slim, Simon suspected he'd weigh considerably less than one hundred and fifty pounds. His hat hung on a peg on the wall behind his chair. Black hair was receding from his forehead, but became much thicker at the top of his head. Then it continued down passing his neck along with the collar of his regimental coat, coming to rest an inch or two below his shoulders. Simon remember everything Mark had told him regarding Captain Williams' service record, and figured he'd possibly been in his late teens when he served during the Civil War.

'I'm not pleased with you Simon,' the Captain said right off. 'I don't know if you're a settler, or a gun runner for Colt. Right this minute I've Lieutenant Cragen going through your wagon. Mostly he'll be looking for pistols and liquor. I've ordered him to only examine and not remove anything he finds.

'Meanwhile I intend on getting to know you better before

the lieutenant reports his findings to me. Words have a way of getting around this fort faster than a horse can jump back away from an angry rattlesnake. As a representative of Colt Firearms, I'd have expected you to present yourself in this office the very day you arrived at Fort Lincoln. Now for my part, I'll set the record straight between you and me. You're a black keeping company with a white woman. That's no never mind to me what so ever. Word has it you ran away from a plantation somewhere down South. That also doesn't bother me one little bit. If you are representing Colt, then I have several questions that I'd like answered.

'As I'm sure you've already heard, I am the only law here at Fort Lincoln. We've a Sutter store here at the fort, and Mark keeps a tight rein on anything that goes out of that store, and who it goes to. Basically that means the Indians here about get no liquor and no firearms. None!

'My soldiers are allowed to buy one bottle of whiskey every other week. I don't tolerate drunken soldiers. If one does become drunk, he can count on one week in the guard house and forfeiture of two week's pay. Plus his loss of right to purchase liquor, or even be caught with it, earns him three months without Sutter store privileges. I'm proud to say that since I took command here, only two of my men suffered the consequences of getting drunk. Finishing their time in the guardhouse, I had them both transferred to a fort a hundred miles south of here. If nothing more, it set the example for the other men assigned to my command. Now if the fact is that you're just spending the winter here, then continuing west, I've no problem with that. But these are the things I need to know. Now in all fairness, I'll give you the floor and you can tell me exactly what you're plans are, and what my Lieutenant is going to report to me after going through your wagon.'

'Well, first off,' Simon said, 'there was no reason for you having my wagon searched. If I learn that my Lady or my son were put out in the slightest by the search, then you and I will be having words, I can assure you. And as for you hauling me in here and saying I should have reported to you as soon as I arrived at this fort, makes no sense whatsoever.

'I am a civilian sir. No different than any of the other civilians that are holding up outside the walls of this fort until spring when we can all get on with our wish to continue westward. When I walked in here, I would have told you that I presently have close to one hundred Colt pistols in my wagon, along with fourteen bottles of liquor. As I say, I'd have told you this if you'd only asked me. While I'm at it, it would have been nice, common custom as I see it, had you greeted me with a handshake and even offered me a seat.

'Just so you'll understand, the pistols are for sale to settlers and Sutter's only. The liquor is mostly for medicinal purposes should that become necessary as our journey continues. I'd hoped to hold on to five liquor bottles to give as gifts to those who have helped me and my family along the way. I started out from Connecticut with fifteen bottles of liquor, but I saw fit to give one bottle along with a pistol to a hotel owner in St. Louis who was kind enough to find my family a small house to rent while we spent a few weeks resting up from our journey, before moving on.

'And now Captain, if you've nothing further to pester me with, I'll be walking out of your office. I sincerely do hope that in the near future, we can speak again on friendlier terms. I like to think I'm not one to go off half-cocked. But like you, I have my fair share of pride, and I don't like being talked down to. I'll say goodbye for now. Do tell your Lieutenant he's welcome to stop by my wagon whenever he pleases.' Having said this, Simon turned and left the building.

Captain Williams leaned back in his chair and stared at the open door Simon had just walked out of. Ever so slowly a smile crossed his face as he thought to himself that he and Simon we're going to get along well. 'The man's got grit, I'll give him that!' he said out loud although there was no one else in the office.

Simon left the fort and walked toward his wagon. Midway, he passed a lieutenant and wondered if this was the man assigned to search his wagon. Darlene was fine when he arrived beside her. Little Simon was thirty feet away, playing with another little boy. Looking inside the wagon, everything appeared to be in its place. 'How did our wagon inspection go?' he asked Darlene.

'Lieutenant Cragen was a real gentleman,' Darlene said. 'He asked me to stay right beside him and told me he was sent by the Captain to inspect our wagon for weapons and liquor only. He even apologized when he put his hand on a pile of our folded clothing, then straightened them out so it appeared they had never been touched.

'Opening the boxes of pistols, he asked me if I knew how many there were. I told him somewhere between seventy-five and one hundred as best I could remember. He asked me to watch as he counted the liquor bottles. He came up with fourteen. He thanked me when he'd finished, and said he hoped he hadn't upset me in any way. He left not three minutes before you showed up.'

Simon chuckled, then told Darlene about his meeting with Captain Williams. 'I do think that we'll have no problem with Captain Williams,' Simon said. 'I'm sure we'll find common ground that we can both be comfortable with. I'll admit he and I got off to a poor start, and I put one hundred percent of the reason for that on Captain Williams. But time will sort everything out as it always does.'

Simon sought out Roger Hawkins, the Wagon Master, and asked about joining his wagon train in the spring.

'So far I've twelve wagons signed up,' Roger said. 'From the little I've heard regarding you, I've been hoping you'd choose to team up with me for the journey west. To my way of thinking, you've got a few pluses going for you.

'First off I'm hoping we get a doctor in our party. My feeling is that next to me, a doctor is the most important person we can have traveling with us. Then word has it you represent Colt Firearms. I can tell you honestly that on two of my trips west we've had some fighting with various Indians. Although every man going west has his own rifle or pistol, it won't hurt knowing we've extra weapons and ammunition with us if it becomes needed.

'I'll be having a look see at your wagon later today and deciding if it's up to the wear, and capable of handling the terrain and distance we'll be going. There are still a couple of Conestoga wagons available that I know of if I feel your wagon falls short of making the trip. And I'll be checking out your horse also. I'll be charging twenty dollars a wagon regardless if it's a farm wagon like you presently have, or it's a Conestoga wagon. As I say, I'll be giving your wagon along with your horse a good going over later today. By week's end, you can decide if you'll take my advice or not. If you do decide to go with me, I'll expect payment in full sometime next week. Any questions you want to ask me?'

'Not off hand,' Simon said. 'Once you tell me your thoughts on my wagon and horse, then I'll be having questions for sure.'

Just at that moment Lieutenant Cragen stepped in front of Simon and announced, 'Captain Williams requests you report to him at your earliest convenience.'

'Well now, that's a welcome change from our last get together,' Simon said to Darlene as he returned to his wagon. 'I won't be long!'

Chapter 7
Making Peace

'**S**imon, I've been thinking since you left here, and the last thing I want is making an enemy of you. Truth is, I hope we can be friends. I've got more than my share of worries just outside these stockade walls than four Captains can handle. Right now safety is my main concern. You've got quite the arsenal of weapons and ammunition in your wagon.

'I'm offering to bring all that, along with every bottle of liquor except one, into this fort. It'll be stored under lock and key and you are welcome to check on it every day if you so desire. I just don't want those supplies of yours sitting in your wagon outside the walls of this fort. I suspect you'll also be getting an additional supply of weapons and ammunition from Colt while you're here. If so, I'd like to put these under lock and key also. Right now everything appears calm and peaceful. But believe me when I say this can change in a heartbeat. As for your possessions, I have no need for them. I feel assured this garrison can defend this fort with the weapons and ammunition we have on hand.

'We also have discipline among the soldiers stationed here, something I don't believe the Indians have among their people. But just to feather my nest so to speak, I've requested a company be assigned here at Fort Lincoln before the snow falls. Now I may not get one hundred men, but I'll gladly take any the army sees fit to send me, be they black or white. Meanwhile, this next month will be a busy time to say the least. I've sixty cord of wood to get inside this fort before winter sets in. Right now the wagons outside are scattered wherever the drivers brought them to a halt. I've spoken with Roger Hawkins, and tomorrow we'll be putting those wagons in a circle for safety sake. Plus that will afford a small measure of privacy to the civilians.

'I suspect you've not witnessed a winter out here. I'll tell you some winters the snow will get as high as the tallest man you see walking about today. Then I've had two winters when we got just a dusting that didn't reach up to a man's knees. Not that it's important to know, but most of the Indians here today, will be gone before winter sets in. Those that have erected teepees will be staying right through the winter. Their teepees are sacred to them. They are comfortable, mobile and regarded as a good mother who shelters and protects her children. To the Indian the teepee is very much alive. Now you think over what I've said regarding securing your guns, liquor and ammunition inside this fort. I'd like your answer by tomorrow, that way, should you decide to accept my offer, when Roger begins moving the wagons tomorrow, we'll slip yours inside the fort, unload the guns, ammo and liquor and have the wagon back outside and under Roger's control without making any fuss.'

'I imagine I don't have to give it any heavy thinking,' Simon said. 'Everything you've said makes perfect sense to me. You or Roger just let me know when you want me to drive my wagon into the fort and it'll be done.'

The following morning, Roger approached Simon and told him his wagon wasn't fit for the journey west. 'After you clean it up a bit, there is a couple that have changed their mind and are looking to return to Pennsylvania. They have already bought a nice Conestoga wagon along with two good horses. I suspect you could work out a trade that would benefit both of you. I don't mind telling you that I believe you actually have the upper hand in this transaction. They realize the Conestoga wagon has no practical use for them in Pennsylvania, whereas your wagon would seem to fit right in.'

At mid-morning Roger Hawkins began positioning the wagons that would be going west. With a nod of his head, he signaled Simon it was time to move his wagon inside the fort. With all the attention focused now outside the fort, Simon passed through the open gates that were quickly closed behind him. In half an hour, his wagon was emptied of guns, ammunition and all but one bottle of liquor. Forty-five minutes after he'd entered the fort, he was positioning his wagon in the circle just left of the fort, at the location indicated by Roger Hawkins. Two hours later he approached Mister Boone who called Pennsylvania his home.

'I'm told you've decided to return home and forget about going further west,' Simon said. 'I have a fine wagon and horse, but my Lady and I haven't decided exactly how far west we'll be going. She is all for seeing the Rocky Mountains, and once we settle on a destination, I'll hopefully be representing Colt Firearms out of Hartford, Connecticut. I understand Roger Hawkins has already told you my wagon will present you with no problem returning to Pennsylvania.' Simon paused and let what he'd said sink in. Meanwhile, he took a long look at the Conestoga wagon Mister Boone and his wife were standing beside.

'I bought this wagon less than two months ago,' Boone said. 'Those have been the longest two months of my life, I can tell you that for sure. I guess, if the truth be known, everything hit my wife about the time we arrived here at Fort Lincoln. She's cried more this past month than I believe she did since she was born. It is a bundle of things. First off it's the kids and grandchildren back home. Then we still own our farm, never did sell it, just told the eldest son to hold on to it until we got settled and decided what we'd do with the place. Had things gone as we'd hoped, I planned on giving our farm to my eldest son. Ten, even fifteen years ago there would be no doubt in my mind that we'd continue going west. But now, and at our age.' Boone just raised his hands as though he was surrendering.

'We had a wagon somewhat like yours when we started out. But I knew it wouldn't get us much further west, not with the rivers and mountains we'd be crossing. I gave your wagon and horse a good looking over, and I can tell you, I can picture it parked in our barn back home sure as I'm standing right here. Now I've a few things to consider. Mainly if we stay here much longer, we'll be here for the winter. But if we can start back for home soon, well you can see the gain for us in that. I paid decent money for this wagon and these horses, but money isn't everything I have under consideration here.'

'Well for my part,' Simon said, 'like you, I guess you could say I'm between a rock and a hard place also. I can go on for a while with the wagon I've got, but eventually, the journey will get the best of me, my horse, and my wagon. So I'll be looking to buy something like you've got standing right here. Now I'll be honest with both you and Mr. Hawkins. I've never driven a two-horse team. So I'm thinking if I bought something now, I just might have the time to accustom myself to doing so before the snow starts flying. And before we go any further, I can honestly tell you that I haven't gotten one red cent from Colt, and won't until I land somewhere and begin representing the company. So considering using the only money we presently have, I'm thinking in the area of twenty-five dollars and my wagon and horse in trade for yours.'

'I was figuring more along the idea of fifty dollars to make the trade,' Boone said.

'This day is almost over and tomorrow will be coming on fast.' Simon said. 'You're looking to get started back east as soon as possible. I'll come up to thirty-five dollars and we can switch out what's in the wagons tomorrow morning,' Simon offered, 'you can be starting east by noon tomorrow if that would be your wish.'

'Done!' Mister Boone said. 'The wife will be pleased and I'll admit I'll be just fine with our decision also. If it's alright with you, we'll switch out everything early tomorrow morning, and hopefully I'll be on my way back home before noon.'

'We've got ourselves a Conestoga wagon and two fine horses to pull it,' Simon said to Darlene as he arrived back at their wagon. 'Early tomorrow, we'll empty this wagon and get it ready for the new owner. Tonight I'll gather all my tools and set them aside. We've still a good stretch of weather ahead of us, and Mr. Hawkins has offered to show me how to manage a two-horse team. Damn! But I can't believe we've got a wagon now that will take us through anything the west has to throw at us.

'I say bring on your Rocky Mountains and whatever else lies ahead of us. I'm going over right now to see Roger Hawkins and tell him I've made the trade.' With that said, Simon started off in the direction of Hawkins' wagon.

Just before noon the following day, Mister Boone pulled Simon's old wagon out of the circle and waved good-bye to acquaintances he and his wife had made during their short stay at Fort Lincoln. Within the hour they were out of sight headed back east to Pennsylvania. Roger Hawkins ordered the other wagons to close up the spot left by the Boone's leaving. He had Simon set his new wagon just off to the left of the circle of wagons, telling people Simon would be learning how to master a two-horse Conestoga wagon. When Hawkins was satisfied with Simon's command of the situation, he'd have him regain the position his original wagon had.

'Now we've a winter to get ourselves through, and I don't doubt but that there might just be other changes within our group.' Hawkins said. 'I've twelve families already signed up to go west with me come spring. Hopefully, we'll get another six or seven, but if we do or if we don't, I'll be keeping the wagon price right where it is. Jeff Moulton only has four wagons signed on so far, so maybe they will eventually see the merit of switching over to our group.'

"The following four weeks were a blur. Each day I spent

at least two hours working with the two horses and making them move the Conestoga wagon from one place to another. That first week Roger sat beside me and passed on a few tricks he'd learned himself over the years regarding handling a team of horses and a large wagon. Also during the time Roger was with me, I found myself taking the new wagon completely out of sight of the fort. It was at these times that Roger Hawkins brought along both a double barrel shotgun and a thirty-thirty Winchester. "

'We won't be going very far, but I want to see you get this team across a stream or two for starters. While we're at it, I've brought these guns along just in case some young bucks see us and figure we'd be easy pickings. Most Indians anywhere near Fort Lincoln are friendly, but safety is always your best watch word. Does your lady know how to handle a rifle?' Hawkins asked.

'Why, she can hit a tin can nine times out of ten at fifty yards with her pistol,' Simon answered. 'As for the rifle I've seen her put three shots out of five into a paper set out at one hundred yards. And what she can do with a riding crop or a ladies short whip, you wouldn't want to know or see!" he said smiling. When not working the wagon or helping Darlene or spending time with their son, Simon spent as much time as possible helping the soldiers chop firewood into useable lengths.

By the end of the month Captain Williams had his sixty cord of wood he needed, stored and covered up against the inside back wall of the fort. With the men's help from those going west with him, Roger also had a decent stack of firewood beside each wagon. 'If this weather holds another week or so,' Roger said, 'the men will try to get another half dozen cord of firewood inside the circle of wagons. Water shouldn't be a problem. There is a good well inside the fort that Captain Williams says we can use.'

"Three days later the first snow of the winter began falling. By dusk, every Indian camped outside, and not having a teepee, had left the area. Two weeks later, November the 10th, thirty troopers arrived to augment Captain Williams' force at Fort Lincoln.

"Lieutenant Cragen had struck up a friendship with Darlene, little Simon, and me. At least once a week, he managed to spend his evening beside our wagon after having eaten supper with us. Often during the day, young Simon, when he spotted his friend, would follow the lieutenant as he made his rounds. Many days he'd arrive back at our wagon fast asleep laying over the lieutenant's shoulder. Martha and Shari often visited with Darlene also. Finally gone was the feeling of uneasiness that had existed when they first met up again at the fort. Martha's husband was fascinated with Simon's wagon and two horses.

'Why, I can't believe the room you've got inside this wagon. Damned if I can't actually stand up inside, and my head still isn't touching the canvas,' James said repeatedly. Simon let the back down and unhinged the two legs allowing the back to act as a table. 'Well, if that don't beat all. Martha, come look here at this table the back of this wagon turns into.' James said. 'Why I've never seen the like of it,' he said over and over again.

'I'm getting somewhat comfortable working with this rig,' Simon said. 'But it involves a few things I hadn't given much thought to before I jumped into buying it. First off, I've now got two horses to feed instead of just one. The wagon itself appears spanking new to me, but I'd like to find and buy at least one extra wheel before we actually start west. Believe it or not, I had two extra wheels with my old wagon. Not that they would even begin to fit this one, but I'll just feel safer once I get another wheel and maybe one or two other items that might need replacing in the future. Roger has told me a couple of horror stories about people who have broken down and had to leave their wagon and most of their belongings behind just because a spare part wasn't available anywhere throughout the wagon train.'

By mid-November, winter had settled in at Fort Lincoln and the surrounding area in earnest. In two days well over a foot of new snow fell. At the end of the week the snow was close to three feet on the level. Settlers were kept busy keeping the snow off the canvas covering on their wagons. Roger Hawkins also advised everyone to lay evergreen pine branches up against the wheels of their wagons so as to protect, and, hopefully, keep them dry throughout the winter.

Jasper Collins, a former Confederate soldier, chose to raise a Confederate flag on the front of his wagon. Within the hour Captain Williams approached Jasper and announced for everyone to hear, 'The war is over and has been for six years now, Jasper! I'm giving you two choices. Fold that flag up and put it away, or haul your wagon away from this fort. I've people here from both the North and the South that have suffered terribly throughout the past war between the states. They don't need to be reminded of the conflict.'

'I have every right to fly this flag,' Jasper said while stepping closer to Captain Williams.

'And I have the authority, along with the right, to throw you off this property,' The Captain said. 'And as for you stepping one foot closer to me, do so and I'll have you placed under arrest before you can spit.'

Jasper, ever so slowly, lowered his hand so that it came to rest just above the handle of his pistol.

'Kansas is a free-state,' the Captain said softly. 'The people of this state voted in 1859 to make it free of slavery. Kansas then entered the union in January of sixty-one. Jasper, you were on the losing side from day one. And at this minute, with your hand almost on the grip of your pistol, I will tell you that before you can place your hand on that revolver, two of my soldiers will shoot you down. Now I've tried to reason with you, but I can plainly see

that isn't possible. So I'll order you to secure your hold-
ings and remove your wagon and family from this property by noon today.'

'You're wrong as wrong can be Captain, and deep down
I think you know it,' Jasper said. 'You Yankees won squat
following your uncalled for invasion into the South. Yes,
Lee surrendered and we were forced to fold our tents and
flag and go home. But look what it's gained you. Why
right here among these settlers you've got a white woman living with a black man who I'm guessing was once
a slave. Now you've got black soldiers standing behind
you with rifles aimed at me. It wouldn't surprise me one
little bit if soon those same soldiers were shooting at you
and the rest of the whites here about. You abolitionists
opened yourself up a hornet's nest, for certain sure, when
you set the Nigger's free.

'I'm telling you straight out, that the blacks and the
Indians are going join up and come down on you just like
you came down on us Southerners. I pray I'm alive to see
it. I believe the South will rise again, because that's our
only hope. But for now, there is just the wife and I. Just
where do you suggest I go at this time of winter.' Jasper
said, spitting out a mouthful of tobacco juice to show his
contempt for Captain Williams and his troops.

'I'd wished you'd given some thought to that before you
put yourself, your wife, this community of settlers, and
my soldiers in the situation you, and you alone, have

caused. My best and only advice is you should consider starting back to North Carolina where you came from. But I can't and don't intend on stopping you from going North, South, East or West just so long as you and your wagon are out of my sight by noon today.' Having said this, Captain Williams turned his back on Jasper and slowly walked back into the fort.

Jasper Collins left Fort Lincoln just before noon, headed back toward Kansas City. Jasper had signed on with Jeff Molton for his westward trip. When he left Fort Lincoln that left only three wagons planning to travel with Jeff. The following day all three signed on with Roger Hawkins. Four days later Captain Williams assigned three troopers to follow Jasper's trail and make sure he was safe.

The snowfall had been less as they rode east. After three days of riding, they were satisfied Jasper and his wife were out of danger and they turned back to Fort Lincoln. Captain Williams thanked them, giving them three days of rest duty. 'I hated like Hell to send Jasper from this fort, but he's the kind who would have pushed and pushed until someone got hurt. I couldn't in good faith let that happen,' the Captain said.

At this point in the interview, Simon stood up, stretched and headed to the coffee pot on the stove where he poured himself a cup. "Would you like a cup of coffee, Miss Jessie?" asked Simon as he held out an empty cup in her direction.

"It will help wash down one or more of those hush puppies that I made for us!"

"Thank you, no, to the coffee", Jessie answered, "I swear I can count the number of times I've drank coffee in the last five years and it wouldn't come up to anywhere near five, but I definitely will have a hush puppy or two!" she said with a smile. "And I happen to know that the editor of The Lexington News, a Mr. John Cook, happens to keep a bottle of Kentucky whiskey right here in the bottom drawer." Jessie slid open the draw and held up a nearly full bottle of Kentucky's Best and two small glasses. "I will need a wee glass of this liquid gold to help wash down my hush puppies! Join me?"

"I do thank you for the offer and I promise to keep your secret! Enjoy your treats. I just feel I'd best get on with my tale so that we don't see ourselves having to get into another day," Simon said as he returned to his chair, sat and enjoyed his own treat.

"Now strange as it may seem, I believe our stay that winter at Fort Lincoln was the happiest time for Darlene and me since we'd met up in Providence," Simon said. "Most days it was colder than a block of ice, while the winds seemed to never let up for a minute. But regardless of the weather, we managed to make the most of it and then some. Between Roger Hawkins and Captain Williams, it was rare when an evening passed without us civilians gathering around a big fire we had burning at the center of the circle of our wagons. Many nights soldiers would join us and some were members of the military band. They could play every type of music you can imagine.

"We often danced late into the night thanks to them. Then on other nights the Indians would come out of their teepees and dance their native dances for us also. At least once a week we'd all eat supper together. It was a pot luck type supper where everyone would bring something to share. I can't say why, but whenever we gathered to eat together, the Indians would stay out of sight.

"Once when a couple of troopers were out on patrol, they managed to shoot a buffalo that they brought back to the fort. Roger Hawkins and Jeff Molton skinned and cut up the animal. Captain Williams gave the hide to the Indians, and had his men erect an affair so the main parts of the animal could be raised up over a fire and turned while it was cooking. The night we ate that Buffalo was the only night I can remember when the Indians joined us.

"Now I'll tell you right here that many people believe that the only good Indian is a dead Indian. Well in the four winter months we spent at Fort Lincoln attitudes changed. I realize we were dealing with friendly Indians, so to speak, but I have to believe if we'd really given the Natives a fair shake, we wouldn't have had all the bloodshed that was to come. Those Indians made toys for many of our children that were with the settlers. They made bows and arrows for the older boys and girls, and took the time to teach them how to use and care for them.

"I learned later they conspired with a soldier, I suspect it was Lieutenant Cragen, but I can't say so for sure. Anyway between his obtaining one of the Captain's shirts that the Indians used to determine size, they presented Captain Williams with a beautiful Buffalo coat from the hide he'd given them. Although the coat had wooden buttons running the full length of the front, another Native lady made a belt covered with beadwork that I was told contained the story of her stay here at the fort.

"As spring drew ever nearer, people began attending to their wagons and horses. I had several chats with the Sutter during our stay, and about a month before we broke camp and started west, he bought two dozen Colt pistols from me at forty dollars each."

'I'd buy another two dozen from you if I had the money.' Mark Hopkins said. 'But if the truth be known, I'd possibly be doing you a disservice. The further west you go, the higher the asking price will be for those pistols. I'll tell you that settlers coming through here, wanting a pistol, will find I'll be asking forty-dollars each for these Colts. And I won't mind telling them they can wait until they get into Colorado or Nebraska before they purchase a pistol. But it won't be spanking new in a box directly from Colt, and they will likely be asking fifty-dollars and upwards, even for a used pistol. Have you decided just where you'll be holding up once you leave here?' Mark asked.

'I'm thinking Denver will be the farthest west I'm considering.' Simon answered. 'Then again, we might just decide to end our westward move sometime soon after we cross into Colorado or maybe Nebraska. Roger has mentioned both.

'Darlene began this trip wanting to see the Rocky Mountains. Well I've seen all the mountains I care to see. To me one mountain looks very much like any other. Since we've been here, we have heard talk about the savages we'll encounter once we get further west. I look at Darlene and our son, and I can't see any reason for exposing them to things that I'm hearing about when it isn't necessary.

'I've been hearing talk of General Philip Sheridan building a fort in the Black Hills. There is also talk of gold in the Black Hills and that the President is going to be sending George Armstrong Custer and the seventh Cavalry into the area within a few months, supposedly, to explore and map the Black Hills. Word has it he'll be taking nine hundred men, along with three Gatling guns and some miners who will determine if there actually is gold in the area.

'The Lakota Sioux are standing by their treaty of eighteen sixty-eight, and Hawkins doubts they will accept miners and settlers, let alone soldiers, having a free run of their land. So now I'm thinking I may go a little further west, but if what I'm hearing is true, we'll either be picking out a place to settle ourselves or turning back and, maybe, giving Pennsylvania a second thought.'

"I gave Captain Williams the money I'd gotten from the sale of the pistols, enclosed in a letter to be mailed to Richard Jarvis at Colt. In the letter that I dictated to Darlene, I recommended that Mark Hopkins, the Sutter here at Fort Lincoln, was a man who could be trusted to represent Colt. The letter also included an accounting of the money resulting from the sale of the pistols. I shared with Richard that the family and I didn't presently have a specific destination in mind, as I doubted we'd be going too much further west.

"On April the third, 1872 Roger Hawkins ordered the circle of wagons to move into a line one hundred yards from where they had spent the winter. The winter snow was gone except for a few places deep in the woods. He'd ridden out two days before and found the trail west to be in good enough shape to support the wagon train. Grasses just off the packed trail were pushing up through the soil and would soon be sufficient for grazing."

'If there is anything you need, I'll be giving you this one last day to acquire it,' Roger said to the group after calling them together. "Captain Williams is willing to forward any letters you may wish to send back east. Mark Hopkins is keeping his Sutter shop open until nightfall for you also. Tomorrow morning we'll be starting west. I'll expect to see a rifle within easy reach of each and every team driver. I've asked three young men from our group to mount up and ride along as I'll be doing. Captain Williams was kind enough to sell us three horses, so the men I've chosen will be riding them.

'Now we'll be a good three or four weeks before we cross into Colorado or as I'm thinking moving further north and entering Nebraska territory. But don't forget for a minute that we could have Indian trouble beginning any-time soon after leaving Fort Lincoln. And I'll say it right here and now. Anyone who desires not to make this trek west for whatever reason, let me know later today and I'll refund your money with no questions asked. Should you decide to return once we've begun, you'll be doing so on your own, and I'll be praying to the good Lord to be watching over you once you leave.

'Last, but not least, a good many of you will find your-selves walking many a day on this journey. So you just might consider an extra pair of shoes when you visit the Sutter shop. If anyone has any questions, I'll be pretty much right here for the rest of the day. I'll see you all again at tonight's meal.' On April fourth 1872 the people at Fort Lincoln awoke to a clear sky and a temperature slightly below thirty degrees. Following a hasty breakfast, Roger ordered the wagons to move out. That first day they covered a little over ten miles which Roger told the wagoneers was exceptional. At the end of the first full week, Simon figured they were almost fifty miles west of Fort Lincoln.

On the afternoon of the fifth day they saw a group of mounted Indians about a half mile away, at the top of a hill off to their right. Roger kept the wagons moving as he rode back along the complete length of the wagon train. 'I'm guessing there are about fifteen Indians on that rise. I also suspect they are young bucks. I doubt they will come any closer to us, but be ready just in case. When, and only IF, I give the word, I'll expect you to circle these wagons as we've practiced earlier.'

Several of these Indians gave out with war whoops while raising their rifles or bows. Ever so slowly they turned and followed the wagon train for about a half a mile keeping their distance. Then they stopped and turned their ponies away from the crest of the hill and rode out of sight.

'Like I said,' Roger announced to each wagon as he rode along the length of his group. 'Young bucks wanting to look like warriors. But we'll keep an eye out for them tonight when we camp. I'll designate two hour watches to stand guard throughout the night. I really don't expect any trouble, but I'd rather be safe than sorry.' The following day the group had covered almost eleven miles when they came upon a stream. Although there was still a couple of hours of light left, Roger chose to camp by the stream for the night.

'There is good water here, and if I remember right, and I'm sure I do, it'll be another three days before we see water again. Once the wagons are circled, I'd advise people to fill their canteens and buckets. When that is done, then we'll let the horses have a go at this water.'

This became a very long night for the settlers. Shortly after dark, wolves began howling. It was a long wailing cry begun by one and soon picked up by the others. Roger walked out from the circle of wagons with a torch in one hand and a rifle in the other and found them to be well over a hundred yards away from the camp site. He counted six that he could see by the reflection of their eyes from the torch light. Within an hour, they moved off and it became silent once again.

'Why didn't you shoot at them?' one of the woman asked as he came back into the circle of wagons.

'No need to,' Roger said as he smiled at the lady. 'They appeared to be mostly pups. Now had they been a grown pack that would be different. I figured they will high-tail it away from here soon enough. I suspect you'll hear their yapping quiet down shortly and they'll move off.' Touching the brim of his hat to her, he walked over to Simon and Darlene's wagon.

'I'll be asking you to keep a sharp eye out starting to-morrow,' Roger said to Simon. 'We'll be seeing more and more Indians in the days to come. This is mostly Pawnee country, but it wouldn't surprise me one bit if we came upon Sioux, Cheyenne or even Crow. And none of them will be putting out the welcome mat for us. You can count on that.

'I've decided I'll be taking us up into Nebraska so you can tell Darlene she'll still be seeing some impressive mountains for sure. Personally I'll be pleased when we can finally make our turn west. I've no intent on going further north into South or North Dakota. We'll strike out for the North Platte, and then I'd be thinking you should be setting your mind on just where you intend to hold up and set down roots. Grand Island, Lincoln, Kearney, you could set down in any one of those locations and I believe you'd do well.

'The railroads are putting wagon trains like this one of ours into the history books. Track is already down in the places I've mentioned. Soon real towns will be springing up, and it'll be trains, what the Indian's call "iron horses" that will be bringing settlers into this country.'

'What changed your mind regarding going into Colorado?' Simon asked.

'I've been thinking we might lose several wagons going through Colorado,' Roger said. 'Between the trail we'd be taking, the twists and turns through the mountains, not to mention the elevations we'd encounter, and as I say, the condition of a couple of these wagons,' Roger shook his head. 'I'm guessing three days, four at the most, and we'd be abandoning at least one wagon for certain sure.

'Then again, there is still a good amount of snow on the trail in Colorado. Hell, one year I remember dealing with wheel-deep snow going through the mountains there in early June. Plus Nebraska offers us several established locations where we can hold up for repairs or just for rest if need be.

'Now I've had to weigh all this in my mind. The trail conditions in Colorado, against the many more Indian tribes we'll be confronting going through Nebraska. And I've been thinking this will possibly be the last wagon train I'll be guiding west. We've great country out here that eventually will be settled proper with houses, churches and schools.

'There is farm land out here that farms in New England can't even begin to hold a candle to. But for these next ten, or maybe even twenty years, settlers will have to deal with the unsavory characters that never should have come west. It'll take time, but sooner than later, the saloons, brothels and gun fighters will fade away.

'And the Indian problems won't be solved overnight for sure. I'm thinking the Army can only do so much. All this will take time to solve before we can attract the number and kind of people this state really needs. Thanks mainly to the Union Pacific Railroad which sold parcels of land to settlers for five dollars an acre, Nebraska became a state in 1867.

'Wyoming is still just a territory, and it's anybody's guess when it will achieve statehood. Colorado is also just a territory. I'm sure statehood will come to both of them eventually; but for the time being, I just feel better about taking these people and their wagons through Nebraska.'

Simon shrugged his shoulders and mused, 'I'm thinking

you just might be right regarding our settling somewhere in Nebraska. I guess I've seen enough mountains to last me a lifetime, and I can't picture much changing were we to go further west. It's been many a mile since we left Hartford, Connecticut and I can already see this trip has taken a toll on Darlene. Our son also needs a real home instead of living in a wagon. We have a house in Providence Rhode Island that a friend said he was leaving to me when he passed on. I'll be checking on that when and if we do head back east.

'I often think back to the time we camped in Pennsylvania by a lake. That is one of the places I'd like to go back to. Then there is a pleasant place in Rhode Island that seems to keep calling me back. As you can see, we have many options should we return east.'

'But I look forward to settling down for a time. I'd build us a home for sure. A home with a good amount of land surrounding it. Then I'd find something to do, maybe a job working for someone, or possibly farming my own land. I'm thinking I'll set my mind to calling this trek to an end at one of the three places you've mentioned. But for now, we can stay put for a while and get our wind back so to speak. I'll see how the gun selling goes, and when we're ready and have decided, we'll start back east if that's in the cards.'

Chapter 8
Crow Indian Trouble

"The following day nearing the noon hour, Roger saw about twenty Indians mounted on their ponies, straddling the trail ahead. These were not the young bucks he'd seen earlier. Raising his hand, he brought the wagon train to a halt. Ever so slowly, he rode down the length of the wagons telling each driver to get the people who were walking inside their wagon, and to keep their rifles ready but out of sight. 'These Indians ahead of us are Crow. I've no idea what they want or what they plan on doing, but I'll figure the worst and hope and pray for the best.'

"Satisfied he'd secured the wagon train, he told the first driver to circle the wagons should anything happen to him while he went forward to talk with the Indians. Roger rode halfway toward the Indians, then brought his horse to a halt and raised his empty right hand high above his head. Several minutes passed before anyone moved. During this time, ever so slowly Roger moved his sight causing little movement of his head as he surveyed the surrounding area for more Indians. Satisfied for the moment that he only faced those before him, he waited patiently for one or more of the Indians to make a move toward him. Eventually two warriors spurred their ponies forward and brought them to a halt directly before him."

'I am Iron Hand of the Crow,' the elder of the two spoke in English. 'I know you, Roger Hawkins.'

'And I know you, Iron Hand,' Roger answered. 'There has never been any anger between us in the years we've known each other. Why do your warriors block our way?'

'Maybe we wish only to trade with your people.' Iron Hand said while he half smiled at Roger.

'These people I lead are settlers bound for Oregon. They have seed they hope to plant, and children they wish to raise in a new land, not here on Crow land.' Roger said.

'I believe your settlers have guns and liquor, we Crow would like to have.' Iron Hand said. 'We have pretty blankets our women have made. These, we are willing to trade also. You are crossing Crow land. Crossing our land cannot be free. I see you have extra ponies, we will trade for these also.'

'I will talk with the settlers and learn if they wish to trade anything they have.' Roger said. 'Weapons and ponies we will not trade. As for liquor these settlers may have a bottle or two among them but if they do, and I don't really know this myself, it is only for taking away pain from an injury or possibly childbirth. I know they won't trade away what little they may have. These settlers are poor. Everything they own is in their wagons. The Crow are rich compared to these people. You have seen the little ones walking.

'The Crow women would give blankets to these young children and moccasins, also, while asking nothing in return. The Crow women are very much like these women. Your warriors are very much like the men on these wagons. These men are not soldiers, but only husbands who will protect their women and children if need be. Let us keep the peace we share between us!

'I will tell these settlers what you have spoken. Give them a day to decide. We will stay on this trail and continue moving west until we speak again.' Saying this, and not waiting for an answer, Roger turned his horse and rode back to the wagon train. The Indians remained where they were for a short time, then turned and rode away.

That evening they circled the wagons for the night's camp, and Roger called the men together. 'I've dealt with Iron Hand in the past, and I know he can go either way depending on how much pressure he gets from his younger warriors. There have been times when settlers I've led have traded with the Crow, and times they have not. Neither have resulted in outright fighting. But make no mistake, the Crow have the upper hand here.'

'I'm not for trading,' Simon said. 'The only items I have available for trade are pots and pans, seed, a handful of hand tools, and, if push came to shove, possibly about a half pound of coffee; but I'll be needing everything I've mentioned as we go further west.'

'How about you others?' Roger asked the group of men that had gathered around him.

'I'm not for trading with them, and I'm not for letting them getting within our circle of wagons,' one man spoke up.

'Just how much territory do these Crow control?' Another asked. 'If tomorrow we move out, how many days do we have before we're out from under them?'

'Once we break camp in the morning, we can expect seeing these Crow by noon. If they keep their distance, they could trail along side of us until they picked a place they felt gave them an advantage,' Roger said. 'I noticed when I talked with Iron Hand, about half his warriors had rifles.'

'Where is the army that's supposed to protect us settlers?' Another asked.

Roger slowly looked over the complete length of the wagon train before he spoke. 'The closest army soldiers might be fifty or even one hundred miles from us. I suppose Iron Hand could give you a more exact distance if he chose to do so. And if you're wondering, the warriors he had with him might be all that he presently has. Then again, he could well have many more that he ordered out of sight when he confronted us. Five days of hard travel, dawn to dusk, would bring us close to Fort Kearney. The closer we are to the Fort, the better the chance patrols sent out from the Fort would have of coming across us. But whether one or five days it could well be a lifetime for us if Iron Hand decides he wants these wagons and horses.

'I'm for us all getting a good night's sleep and hitting the trail at dawn tomorrow. If and when we come up against Iron Hand again, I suggest we instantly circle these wagons, unhitch the horses and tether them inside our circle close to each wagon they belong to. I'll ride out and talk with Iron Hand again when I see we're secure. Maybe we'll be lucky if he sees a show of strength on our part. But my hope will still be that he'll wait until he believes he's on better ground before he confronts us again.'

Roger walked around slowly inside the circle of wagons stopping now and then to chat individually with various couples. When he came upon Simon, he took him behind his wagon and beckoned Darlene to join them. 'Simon, tomorrow just may be a bad day for us. I'm hoping it won't, but I've been down this trail more times than I wish to remember, and I've dealt with Iron Hand in the past. So tomorrow, or whenever we're confronted by these Crow, I'll ride out and try to reach a peaceful agreement with them that will let us continue on our journey.

'Two things I'll be asking of you. First off, if anything happens to me when I'm with the Indians, I'll expect you to take out Iron Hand immediately. The Indians don't do well without their chief. Taking him out will give our people precious time.

'You once told me Darlene could hit a target set out at one hundred yards three times out of five shots with a rifle. I'm counting on you doing better. But I've an extra rifle that I'll be loaning Darlene. If you miss with your first shot, I'll trust Darlene will not need a second bullet to do the job I'm giving you. Have you any problem with what I'm asking?' Roger asked Darlene.

'None!' Darlene answered. 'But what will we all do without you guiding us?'

'The trail ahead is well worn and it will bring you to Fort Kearney within a week. But as I said,' Roger continued. 'Should the Crow or any Indians over-run this wagon train, I want to go to my grave knowing your wagon with the guns and ammunition, along with the liquor, will be blown to Kingdom Come long before they lay hands on it. And at Fort Kearney there will be others who will guide you on further west.'

"The following morning Roger formed the wagons in line and started them on the trail leading toward Fort Kearney. The morning passed without sight of Iron Hand or any Crow Indians. The settlers did not stop at noon, but continued on until one hour before sunset. Once again they formed their defensive circle with their wagons, unhitched their horses and brought them inside. Fires were started, and soon the air was filled with the odor of cooking. Roger posted a rifled guard at the rear of every second wagon with orders not to shoot until he himself had been called to assess the situation. The night passed quietly, and dawn broke to overcast skies promising rain."

'Normally I'd stay right here for another full day,' Roger said as the men hitched up the horses to their wagons. 'But time isn't on our side to my way of thinking. The Crow don't give up without a fight. The very least I'd expect from them is to see them attempt to cut out one of these wagons. Then again I can think of a dozen reasons Iron Hand could be holding off. Possibly he's waiting for more warriors he's summoned. Maybe, he knows of cavalry close by in the area. Then again he may have already picked the place he chooses to confront us. Whatever his thinking, we'll be moving out in about fifteen minutes. Check your wagons, look to anything you think could use attention or repair.'

After an hour on the trail, the sky opened up with a downpour. At mid-morning just as the rain was letting up, the fifth wagon in line had a rear wheel break free from the axel, bringing the complete wagon train to a standstill. Roger rode back, dismounted and examined the damage. 'It's not just the wheel, the axel is split through almost its complete length.' Roger said. 'You can save the wheel as it can be used on another wagon; but this wagon is finished. I'll ask you to team up with someone and transfer whatever you can into their wagon. I suspect others will take some of your items also. This wagon will be staying right here. I expect to have us moving again within a half hour at the most, so get to it!'

"True to his word, Roger had the wagon train moving well within the hour. The abandoned wagon had been pushed off the trail leaving it on its side, but empty. Just at dusk as Roger was circling the wagons for the night, the Crow appeared once again. When Roger was satisfied the people and wagons were secure, he nodded toward Simon, then mounted his horse and rode out to talk with Iron Hand."

'You have lost one wagon,' Iron Hand said. 'But you left nothing in it for my people. Not even a hammer or a file did my warriors find. Tomorrow we will take the wagon anyway. But we want the horse that was pulling the wagon. And we also want two of the extra horses you have. Give us these, and we will let you pass over our land.'

Roger leaned off to the side of his mount and spit on the trail. 'Hear what I say, my friend. We will trade for the horse that pulled the broken wagon. I'll ask the settler and his wife what they will take in trade for their horse. The other horses we will not trade. But I will give you instead a promise. Once I deliver these settlers to Oregon, I will guide no more wagons through your lands. This is my only offer.

'I honor the Crow and do not wish to fight. But as you protect and listen to your people, I also must protect and listen to these settlers. I will go back and talk to those who own the horse that pulled their wagon and learn if they will trade it away, and if so, what they will expect as a fair trade.'

Turning his back on the Crow, Roger rode back to the circled wagon train. Talking with the people who had lost their wagon he explained what Iron Hand wanted. 'You decide what we should ask for. For my part I want nothing from these savages. But if it will allow us to get to Fort Kearney without a fight, so be it.'

Once again Roger rode back to where the Crow Indians were waiting. 'The settler and his wife had hoped to keep their horse so they could continue west. But they are willing to trade the horse for ten Crow blankets, and free passage over this Crow land,' Roger said.

'Three blankets and all the whiskey from the wagons!' Iron Hand demanded. 'And I still want the two other horses also.'

'I'm thinking many of your braves will die soon, as will some of these settlers.' Roger said. 'And the blood of all who die here will be on your hands. So now I will give you my offer. You can have one of your warriors deliver the blankets to Fort Kearney, and you will be given the horse from the broken wagon there. There is no need for you to attack these settlers.

'Tomorrow I will lead these settlers on toward Fort Kearney. You are a brave chief. Take your warriors away from this place, and let these poor people continue on in peace. No man should die for a horse or a blanket, or even over a hammer. I have spoken for these settlers. No more need be said. I leave you in peace.' Saying this, once again Roger turned his mount and began riding back to the circle of wagons. Within twenty steps, he felt an arrow fly past his right side. Leaning forward and placing his head against the side of his horse's head, he spurred his mount into a gallop. At the same moment he clearly heard the report of rifle fire coming from the direction of the wagons.

Simon saw the Indian draw his bow and took aim, firing instantly. Darlene fired a second later hitting Iron Hand in the shoulder and knocking him from his horse. The Indian who had shot the arrow at Roger was already dead as he collapsed on his pony. When the horse moved this Indian fell to the ground.

Several Crow jumped down from their horses and ran to their chief. Roger, meanwhile, had reached the safety of the circled wagons. Dismounting he ordered no one to shoot as he looked beyond the wagons at the Crow.

Simon stepped beside Roger and said, 'I shot the Indian who I saw draw his bow and send an arrow at you. Darlene fired a second later and hit Iron Hand who fell from his horse.'

For several minutes all watched as the Indians gathered around their chief. Slowly, but clearly being helped to his feet, Iron Hand leaned against his pony. Roger could see Darlene had hit the chief high in the left shoulder. There was no doubt that the Indian Simon had shot was on the ground dead.

'Now this would be the perfect time for the cavalry to arrive with their flag flying and blowing their bugles.' Roger said. 'But that only happens in the dime novels people back east are reading. We'll just have to stay put and wait this out. Iron Hand will be the one who decides what happens next.'

Stepping over to Darlene, Roger put his arms around her and gently kissed her. 'Lady, you may not know it, but you just might have saved the lives of all these people with your shooting today. Thank you! Now I can't say for sure, but I do believe these Crow will not attack us. They will take their chief to the nearest village and tend to his wound.'

Turning back to Simon, Roger grasped Simon's hand in both of his. 'That arrow was so close I could hear its feathers cutting the air as it passed my ear. The two shots you both fired will be talked about among the Crow for many a month to come. They thought they were just dealing with settlers. But two shots, and two hits will have them thinking this over again. I do believe as I've said, Iron Hand will not attack us. They will return to their village and lick their wounds. As long as Iron Hand lives and does not die from his wound, we'll consider ourselves safe.'

"Three days later Roger brought the wagons to a halt just outside the gates of Fort Kearney. Once again Roger formed the wagons in a protective circle before he left the settlers and entered the fort to speak with the commander."

Roger was well known to Captain Mark Turner. Mark rose from behind his desk and shook hands with Roger before either of them spoke a word. 'How was your crossing?' the Captain inquired.

'We encountered a band of Crow Indians who took matters into their own hands by attempting to kill me as I rode back to the wagons!' Roger answered. 'I was saved from certain death by two very special people.'

'Where did this happen?' the Captain asked as he took his seat behind his desk and directed Roger to a chair.

'About three or four days out,' Roger said. 'We'd been confronted by Iron Hand and about fifteen to twenty of his warriors for a couple of days before the shooting happened. He was after horses, liquor, guns, anything he thought we might trade with him. But trade or no trade, He intended to take what he wanted regardless. One family lost their wagon due to a split axel and a wheel that came off. Iron Hand wanted the horse that had pulled that wagon. We'd left the wagon on its side, shoved off the trail. I'm thinking we'd have had one serious fight on our hands if one of his braves hadn't jumped the gun and shot an arrow at me as I was returning to the wagon train after speaking with Iron Hand. This couple I want you to meet ended the situation with two shots. The man killed the Indian who fired the arrow at me, and his lady hit and knocked Iron Hand off his pony a second later. Now these Indians were a good eighty to one hundred yards distant from the wagons when this couple fired. I thank the good Lord I had them along with me. I honestly doubt any of us would have survived had things not gone as they did. I guess I don't have to tell you that the Crow are no doubt somewhat like a hornet's nest right now. I advise you to double your men when they go out on patrol until things calm down.'

'How long will you be holding up here at the fort before moving on?' Mark asked.

'I figure a week, two at the most. It'll depend on if these settlers can find themselves another wagon, or if they'll be content with doubling up?' Roger said.

'Getting a new or used wagon should prove no problem,' Mark advised. 'The Union Pacific are laying track to beat the band, and they have a supply depot not five miles from this very fort. I've been out there several times, and I swear they have a dozen extra wagons just sitting there doing nothing. I'm sure your folks will be able to come up with a wagon with little or no problem at all. In fact I'll send one of my men out to that depot within the hour to advise them of the Crow situation. Paul Atkins is the man in charge out there. He'll want to know about your incident with Iron Hand so as to advise his crew to be aware and alert.

'A good ninety present of his workers are Chinese. How this information will set with the crew I haven't a clue. And by the way, I believe I've two families here that are looking to move west. I'll put them in touch with you, and you can possibly work something out with them.'

Going back to the settlers, Roger informed them that unlike Fort Lincoln, the sutler shop here was open every day. 'Now I haven't been in the store as of yet, so I can't say anything as to what's available inside. But you'll have plenty of time to check everything out as I figure we'll be staying right here one full week, possibly two.'

The following day Simon entered the sutler's store. It was a little larger than the previous sutler's store at Fort Lincoln but not by much.

'James Cody is my name, and I've been here at this fort going on two years now,' he said as he shook Simon's hand. 'Clothes and grub is my main seller. I do have a few rifles from time to time, mostly cast off from the army. I have no contract with Winchester or Remington. I imagine I'll be closing up shop here by the time this year runs out. With the railroad being so close, people are starting to settle here-a-bout. Soon I expect someone will open a general store, and that will be the end for me.

'It's a good location for settling, with the fort close by and we'll soon have a railroad connected all the way back to St. Louis. I imagine the railroad will keep right on pushing west until it runs up against the Pacific Ocean. I can tell you it's a far cry from when I first arrived here, and that's the truth. The fort is named after General Stephen W. Kearny. His son Philip was a Colonel who fought in the Civil War and was killed at the battle of Chantilly in eighteen sixty-two. People now are settling north of the Platte River in an area we call Dobytown. As we're right on the Oregon Trail I guess I've seen over a dozen wagon trains of settlers come through here.

'Most have continued on, but some as I've said, have settled themselves within a mile or two from this fort. Hell, other than for the damned Indians, there is everything a body could ask for right here. I know of people who have shot Elk or deer right in their own backyard. Then, you can't find a better fishing river than the Platte. We're a little over two thousand feet high here, so the soil is rich and ready for farming.'

'Well, I just may be settling here also. My Lady and I have a child who has known nothing but a wagon as a home for way too long, he is going on four years old now,' Simon said. 'And if I do set down roots here, I'll be representing Colt Firearms out of Hartford, Connecticut. I'll only be dealing in Colt revolvers to start, but from what I'm hearing from you, I just may branch out and see how I do.'

The second full day Simon was at the fort, he borrowed the horse from the owner of the lost wagon and rode out to the Dobytown area. It was less than two miles when he came upon the first cluster of settler's houses. There were only six families that he could see, and it appeared each had located their house on about five acres of land. The houses were a sight to see. Some consisted of the basic structure being nothing more than a crate he suspected the owner had bargained for from the Union Pacific railroad.

Off in the distance he could see another seven or eight homesteads. There were no roads winding between these houses. Instead, the grass was matted down making clear pathways from property to property. Simon counted seven trees among the first group of settler's homesteads, and guessed another eight or nine were standing near the homesteads further off. Other than for these, the closest trees were a good quarter of a mile in the distance. Many trees had been cut down and lay stacked together off to his right. Eventually they would be trimmed, and sawed into boards in order to make proper buildings. Approaching the first settler he spied, Simon introduced himself.

'And I'm Bert Webster," the man said as he reached up and shook Simon's hand. "I hale from Massachusetts originally, but couldn't abide living one floor above a butcher shop and sharing a four-hole privy out back with people I didn't really know. I left home when I was fourteen. Settled myself in the Mohawk Valley in New York that first time. Then when the war started up, I figured it was time I moved on. I didn't give a hoot about the fighting, but just knew New York would be drafting me if I stayed put.

'So I took myself off to Ohio, where I met my wife. With the war now going full -blast and no end in sight, we bought ourselves a wagon and headed out here. The wife has given birth to a son and a daughter in that wagon. We've been right here a little over a year now, and I've become partial to this place.

'The soil is good, and we grow just about everything ourselves that we need, with some extra to share with our neighbors. We've a good deep well that gives us pure clean water. Now when I say deep, I didn't have to dig down more than fifteen feet to strike a solid vein of water.' he asserted as he passed a ladle of clear, cold water for me to drink. 'Here! Have a taste of the best water west of the Mississippi River!'

'Every place you can see has a well just like ours. We cleared most of the trees from our land because of the Indians. I left a half dozen trees standing, mostly for shade. But I figure it would have to be a mighty skinny Indian, and, only one at that, to try and hide behind one of these trees.' Bert laughed as he said this. 'Truth is, once the Indian problem is solved I'll be planting an apple orchard beside my place. We're looking to build ourselves a saw mill so we can all build proper houses.'

'How has the Indian problem been living out this far from the fort?' Simon asked.

'We've seen Cheyenne and some Sioux come by once or twice, but Mr. Charbonneau is living with a Pawnee woman, and I think that's what keeps the peace for us, so to speak. He was a trapper long before the fort was ever built here. He can talk with just about any Indian within a hundred miles of here regardless of their tribe. I guess he's even talked with the Crow when he's come across them, or them across him. I personally don't trust any of them. But then again Lilly, that's the Pawnee woman who lives with Charbonneau, is one of the nicest people you'll ever meet.

'It's like my wife always says, there is good and bad people in everyone you meet. Right following the war there was a problem with the Confederates that came here. But the soldiers put a stop to their shenanigans right off. I don't know if we've any of them living around here now. I suspect a few have joined the army. As for the others, I'm pretty sure they've moved on. You thinking of settling here?'

'I'm giving it some thought, I'll admit that. I understand there is some good land north of the Platte River. And I like the idea of the Union Pacific Railroad being just a stone's throw away. I'll hope to get back out here in a few days, and visit with some of your neighbors.' Simon said as he again shook hands with Bert.

"Early the following morning five Crow Indians arrived at the gates of Fort Kearney as a Trooper called out, 'Corporal of the guard, advise the commander, we have Crow Indian guests at our gate.'

"Hearing these words shouted out, a good twenty soldiers quickly climbed the ladders and from the top of the stockade wall looked out at these Indians. None of the Indians possessed rifles, and only two had a bow hanging at the side of their ponies. While they waited to see the fort's commander, two of the Indians looked over at the settlers standing beside Roger's wagon train. Soon the gate was opened and Captain Mark Turner approached the Indians.

'What brings the mighty Crow warriors here to the fort, and where is your leader Iron Hand?'

'Iron Hand has been hurt and needs the white's medicine. The bullet that struck him did little damage, but now Iron Hand has the fever and we cannot make it go away.'

Mark turned to the orderly standing beside him and told him to fetch the fort's doctor. 'Did you take the bullet out of your Chief?' Mark asked.

'The bullet is out, but we think a small piece of his shirt remains in the wound. Our medicine man took pieces of the shirt out, but some threads still are believed to remain.'

At this point the doctor arrived carrying his leather medical bag. Mark explained the situation to him, and the doctor immediately rummaged in his bag pulling out four white pills and a vile of liquor. Getting Mark's permission he stepped up to the Indian who had done the talking. 'Give Iron Hand two of these pills today and then pour half the liquor into the wound. Tomorrow give him the other two pills and pour the rest of the liquor into the wound. If by the third day he is not well, and the fever is not broken, you must bring him here to the fort for me to examine.'

'It was my brother who died when our Chief was shot.' Saying this, the Indian once again looked over at the people standing by the wagon train. Having had his say, the Crow Indians turned their ponies and left the fort's area.

'Let us hope that this is the end of it and Iron Hand recovers,' Mark said. 'I don't like it one bit, and that's for sure. I don't trust or like Iron Hand. But the devil you know is often better than what comes after he's gone.' Giving a wave to Roger, he indicated the wagon leader should follow him into the fort.

'You told me that when the shooting started, the Indians were eighty to one hundred yards away.' Mark said. 'Do you think the Indian doing the talking today could have seen who in your party did the shooting? I noticed he gave a good looking over at your settlers a couple of times while I spoke with him.'

'It's possible', Roger said, 'but to be honest I doubt it. Simon and his lady both fired from behind their wagon. And today, as soon as I saw those Crow approach the fort, I had Simon and Darlene stay out of sight, while the other settlers milled around in plain view out of curiosity. Then again the distance along with the swiftness of what happened along with it being overcast, No I don't believe the Indians know who fired at them. My best guess is that for a time after the shooting, many of the settlers themselves didn't know who actually fired the shots.'

'Well we'll just have to wait a day or two and learn if Iron Hand recovers. If he does, I think that will be the end of it. He's been bit hard once by your settlers, I suspect he'll be glad to see them leave the area. He well may challenge a future wagon train, but I seriously doubt he'll give any consideration to following yours when you head out. Oh, and by the way, I believe you'll have two new couples wanting to sign on with you before you head west.' Mark said.

Later that morning Simon rode over to the Union Pacific depot office and introduced himself to Paul

Atkins. 'I'm giving some thought to settling here, and if I do I'll be representing Colt Firearms out of Hartford, Connecticut. Now I'll be up front with you, my Lady is white and we've known each other since we were in South Carolina. We parted ways and came across each other the better part of a year later in Providence, Rhode Island. One thing led to another and now we're a family. Our son is four now and I'm thinking it's time he learns that a Conestoga wagon is not a home.

'I'm thinking of building our home somewhere on the north side of the Platte. I've scouted out several couples who have settled in what's called Dobytown, northeast of the Platte and the fort. Now while I like the folks there, I don't intend on starting a home here living out of a Union Pacific cast off crate. I'm wondering if it is possible that I could buy enough milled lumber from Omaha and have it shipped here by train before you and your crew move further west?'

'When was the last time you met with Richard Jarvis?' Paul asked. Before Simon could answer, Paul offered that he himself grew up in Hartford and knew Richard well. 'As to when we'll be moving on west, I suspect it'll be next spring before we chose a place further on to set up shop. There is still a heap of work to be done right here and in the next ten or so miles before winter sets in.

'This coming winter I figure to hold up right where we are. And regards milled lumber, I'll soon be ordering a load myself as I intend on building a good-size shed so that when I do move on I can dissemble and move it to our new location. You draw up a list of what you'll be needing, and I'll send it along with mine sometime in the next two weeks. I figure we'll have our lumber delivered here in four, maybe five weeks tops.

'Now if I were you, I'd consider going a little further west to Lexington. I scouted that area out about a month ago. It's prime land for a fact. And we'll be building a spur there next season for sure.

'By the way,' Paul said lowering his voice. 'What I just said about the spur is private information. Anyone looking at our Union Pacific maps will not see a spur shown at Lexington. Back before the war, Lexington was just a frontier trading post originally called Plum Creek. Lexington was actually founded in 1871 but I see a lot of potential for growth in that particular area.

'Now Lexington is less than a week west of Kearney by wagon, but you've a horse and the time to ride out and check the area out for yourself. Any lumber you order from Omaha, we can leave right on the railroad car and deliver it close to a site you may choose to build at. You'll still be right on the Platte River, and I suspect in no time at all Lexington will grow into a fine city leaving places like Kearney in the dust. Anyway, it's something for you to be thinking about.'

That night Simon related to Darlene everything Paul had told him. 'And what are you thinking?' Darlene asked?

'I'm thinking that either I should ride out to Lexington and look the area over, or that we should go out there together in our wagon and check things out. We've traveled the Oregon Trail enough as far as I'm concerned. Personally I'd like to settle down and get on with raising a family.

'All the way back from the depot, all I kept thinking about was building us a home with a garden area alongside where we could raise any crops we needed. I'm thinking we might even turn the front room into a small store where I could have a go at selling Colt pistols.' Simon answered.

'I'll admit,' Darlene said, 'I've about had my fill of living out of a wagon. And with this recent Indian shooting, I'm not all that thrilled with the thought of our going further west, and dealing with what I've been told are worse Indians to come. I'll trust your judgement and let you ride out there and look the area over.

'Just so you'll know, I'm excited about settling down and getting on with adding to our family. I'm happy you've decided to order milled lumber for our home, and I can't believe you've already established a pathway to having it delivered to where we'll be building. When are you thinking of leaving?'

'I'm thinking tomorrow, or the day after,' Simon said. 'Tonight we'll draw up a list of what we figure we'll be ordering regarding lumber from Omaha. Roger has said he plans on staying here with the wagon train for two weeks. I suspect I can ride out, check out the area, and be back here in five or six days. But let me ask you something else to be thinking about. If I find nothing of real interest at Lexington, would you consider our going back East? Not Rhode Island or Connecticut, but possibly somewhere in the country that we came through?

'I'll hold our lumber list until I return. Paul said it would be a couple of weeks before he sent his list, and ours would go with his. I think this will give us the time to think everything through and make a decision we can both live with and feel good about.'

'I'll wait until you get back after checking out Lexington. But I already know if it isn't Lexington, I'm all for returning east. You've often spoken of that small town in Rhode Island. Well I'll tell you now, I've thought and actually dreamed about that place by the lake in Pennsylvania where we stayed. So to my way of thinking we have several options open to us.' Darleen squeezed Simon's hand and smiled in her special way, 'Don't be too long.'

The following day Simon headed out for Lexington. The country he rode through appeared much the same as he'd found when they had arrived at Fort Kearney. On the evening of the first day's riding, he believed he'd arrived at Lexington. Only one homestead stood a good two hundred yards back from the Platte River. Seeing a man standing in what appeared to be a garden area, he rode over to him and began to dismount.

'Hold it right there feller,' the man in the garden said while at the same time raising a rifle up that had been leaning against a log. 'Step closer so I can see you better. These eyes aren't what they use to be by a long shot, but I've had more Indians coming around my place these last couple of weeks than I've had in the last year. And not just Cheyenne and Sioux. Why, just yesterday, or was it the day before, I'll be damned if I can rightly remember to keep my days straight lately.

'Anyway two Crow Indians walked right into my house. I was out here in the garden hunkered down, and they didn't see me. They carried off a few things. I don't know what all they took, but then they started a fire against the side of my place.

'Well they rode off, and I beat it over to the fire and put it out after it had blackened half the wall. That's why I have this rifle out here in the garden with me today. Now I'll be asking, what's your business out here today? You working for the railroad that's coming through here?'

'My name is Simon, and I guess you could say I'm a settler much like yourself. My family and I are with a wagon train that is presently resting up at Fort Kearney. I've also heard the Union Pacific will be coming right through here sometime next spring or summer. I figured I'd ride out and check the land out to see if I wanted to set roots down here, or continue on with the wagon train that will be going all the way to Oregon. I'm partial to locating somewhere along this Platte River, and I'm hearing also that this particular area just may become a main station on the railroad line.'

Lowering his rifle, the old man reached out and shook Simon's hand. 'First time I've seen a black man that wasn't a soldier,' he said. 'Name's Thomas, and I settled here over ten years ago. I claim all the land in sight from right where we are standing. But I haven't filed any papers with the state as of yet. I guess I won't be filing any claim to this land. Too many Indians around here for my liking. That first year or two I settled here I never saw so much as one Indian. I'm telling you that a lot has changed in these past couple of years. And I can't say anything has changed for the better either.

'This here garden isn't much to look at, but I manage to get enough carrots, beets and even some corn out of it every year. I could get a lot more vegetables if I worked it more, but basically you could say I'm old and a meat eater. Now the Platte often has so many ducks on it, I'm thinking you could walk across it stepping from duck to duck and not ever get your feet wet. Elk, Moose and Deer just about trip over one another there are so many. And from time to time I've seen my share of Bear also.

And the fishing is good just about year round also. If it wasn't for the Indians, and my being as old as I am, I'd consider starting over, and build me a proper cabin with a decent garden. But I feel my time is running out, so I'll just make do with what I have.'

Simon once again told Thomas that he was just looking the area over, trying to decide if he wanted to settle locally. 'My Lady and I have a four year old son going on five. Today I'm thinking its time I decide if we settle here, or consider moving with the wagon train further west.

'We're also considering heading somewhere back east. We came across some real pretty country getting this far and haven't forgotten some of the places we passed that now we're thinking what just might be the better of the choices we're facing. From what I'm seeing this place has a couple of good things going for it.

'With the railroad coming through, it won't be long before a real town springs up close by. Then there is Fort Kearney only a little ways away. I figure once people start settling around here, soldiers will become as thick as bee's around a hive. I'm thinking that alone will go a long way to solving the Indian problem.

'Thomas, if you don't mind, I'll just have a look see around, and try to get a picture in my mind of what this place could look like in a couple of years. I'll follow along the Platte River a piece, and check back with you before

I return to my family. Meanwhile you be keeping a sharp eye out. We had a serious run-in with some Crow a week or so ago and killed one Indian, and wounded their chief. The Captain at the fort is waiting to see if the chief survives. Meanwhile, I suspect it's best to lay low until things blow over.'

Simon walked his horse slowly along-side the Platte River. Off in the distance to the northwest, he could see snowcapped mountains. But here the ground was level and it appeared it would not take much to clear an acre or two for planting. Trees throughout the area would provide firewood for a lifetime and then some. He wondered exactly where the Union Pacific would be laying their track. Stopping, he looked out across the Platte River. In the four or five hundred yards he'd crossed, he'd come upon many animal tracks.

Looking over the area once again, he figured out where he thought not only where the tracks would be, but also where eventually a train station would be built. Turning and going back along the line he'd traveled, he came to a spot that seemed to call out to him. The ground here rose up, so there would be decent run off of rain and snow melt. He figured where he stood was a little over two hundred yards from the river. And being on the north side of the Platte, he could plainly see the opposite side of the river was much lower. Mounting his horse once again, he returned to where Tom was now splitting firewood.

'This is good land,' Simon said as he climbed down from his horse and stepped close to Thomas. 'I can picture a decent size town springing up here once the railroad comes through. I'll be heading back to my boy and my lady, and we'll be talking well into the night about what I've seen here. I do know one thing for sure after looking this place over, if I have my way, we won't be going on toward Oregon with the wagon train. To my way of thinking this is as far west as we'll be going. And I'm not ruling out our turning around, and back tracking possibly all the way to Pennsylvania. But one way or the other, I hope to get back out and see you again regardless of what we decide.'

Two days later, just after the noon hour, Simon got down and tied his horse to the side of his wagon. 'Well, I've seen the land up Lexington way,' Simon said to Darlene as he gave her a hug, 'and in all fairness, I guess I've got some good, and some bad news to share with you.

'First off the good news, I doubt we could find a better site to settle ourselves in than the area I've seen these past couple of days. There is only one settler there now, an older gentleman named Thomas. And the land is very much like where we camped for a few days by that lake in Pennsylvania.

'Wild game is as thick as the grass growing at our feet. I'm talking fish, ducks, deer, moose, birds of every kind, and even bear. You can see snowcapped mountains off in the distance, and with the Union Pacific railroad to be cutting its route through that area by next summer, I can almost picture the town that will spring up before little Simon is eight years old. Clearing the land for a homestead with a good-sized garden shouldn't take us more than a month.'

Simon picked up his son who'd come running to him from where he'd been playing with other children. Holding the boy on his shoulder, he and Darlene moved to the opposite side of the wagon where it was shady. Within minutes his boy ran back to the children he'd been playing with.

'Now for the negative points of our settling there,' Simon said as both he and Darlene sat down. 'The Indians are my only real concern. The day before I arrived a couple of Crow stole items from Tom's cabin and then set fire to the outside of the cabin's east wall. They didn't see Tom hunkered down in his garden area, and as soon as they left he ran over and put out the fire. Tom also told me that since he'd settled there, he'd seen Cheyenne and Sioux also. But he did say he had no trouble with the Indians until a couple of days ago when as I said, two Crow showed up. He said he thought of shooting them, but his eyesight isn't what it used to be, and he was just thankful they took whatever it was they took, and left.'

'And now that you've seen the area, what is your opinion?' Darlene asked.

'I guess I'd like to think on it a day or two before I decide. As I say, there is a powerful lot in favor for us settling there. We've the fort right here for one thing. And with the railroad coming through there next spring or summer, the area is bound to grow.

'We've also got the connection with Paul heading up the Union Pacific locating there, and the offer of getting finished lumber delivered right to our site by train. I guess my only real concern is the Indian situation. But you know, as we said before we started out on this journey, Southerners, soldiers, Indians, animals and what have you, I figure we can handle whatever we come across. Now what about you?' he asked, 'what are you thinking?'

'I'm not for going on any further. I realized that the night after you left to check out Lexington. And if the area is what you report it to be, I'll admit I'm sorely tempted to go and see it for myself. As for the Indian situation, I do believe it will be solved throughout this area completely in two, maybe three years at the most. I've already shot one Indian, I guess if pushed into it, I could shoot a few more if need be. Not that I want to mind you, but if we decide to settle in Lexington, then that will be our home. From everything I've seen, the Indians haven't really done anything with all this land. They've had their chance, now if we, and others thinking like we do, want to plow and farm the land and build towns even better than the ones back east, well I say it's our turn and it's our time now,' Darlene said.

'Tomorrow I'll talk with Roger and tell him our thoughts. I'll find out just how long he intends on remaining here. If we've time, you and I will ride out and look over the area I've just told you about. What about little Simon? I mean we can go in the wagon if we've the time, but if we both just rode, it would make the trip quicker and shorter,' Simon said.

'I'll check with Martha and Sheri,' Darlene said. 'I'm sure they'd be happy to watch our boy while we're gone. But again, it will depend on what you hear from Roger regarding the amount of time we'll have.'

'Captain Turner tells me he's expecting a stage with dispatches coming through here in one week,' Roger told Simon when they talked. 'I'm thinking we'll head out the day after that stage arrives. Who knows, there may be letters for some of the settlers, and maybe even something coming for me. Anyhow, another week resting up here won't hurt us one bit as far as I can see. I'm hearing you're thinking of leaving us and having a go at settling along the Platte River up Lexington way. Am I hearing correct?'

'I guess you know I've already been up that way. Now based upon the time you'll be staying here, Darlene would like to go back up with me and look the area over again. We're thinking if we both rode and left the wagon here, we'd make better time and be back sooner. We've friends willing to watch our son, so it comes down to when you are starting the wagon train west, and if we've time enough.' Simon said.

'Damn!' Roger said. 'I really hate to lose two good marksmen at this stage of the trip. But here, or somewhere between here and Oregon, it would be just the same. And I've seen the area you'll be looking at. I'll admit it's the sort of place I'd consider myself. Now add in the fact the railroad will be going right through there, and I have to believe you'd have yourself a winner.

'You and Darlene ride out first thing tomorrow morning, and I'll expect you back here not a day over five days. I'll also be keeping an eye on the little feller while you're gone. I'll have a chat with Captain Turner and see if he just might decide to send a patrol out that way also, since we haven't heard how the medicine worked on Iron Hand. If the people here ask why we're staying put, I'll give them the same reasons of the expected Stage and not knowing Iron Hands' condition. I wish you and Darleen a safe journey.'

Chapter 9
The Calm Before the Storm

"Early the following morning Darlene and I saddled up and headed out to the area known as Lexington where we arrived the following afternoon. Everything was just as I had described. The water of the Platte River appeared ripple-free like a mill pond. Darleen was delighted when she guessed that at least one hundred ducks were floating on the river within her sight. As we brought our horses to a halt, half a dozen mule deer that had been drinking at the water's edge, ran off disappearing into the distant, thick woods off to the west. I pointed out where I suspected the railroad tracks would be put down and where I thought of locating our cabin.

"I pointed out where I thought a train station might be built near where a cluster of large rocks stood. If so, we could expect to see a decent-size town develop within a couple of years. But even if I was wrong, and the station was built a mile in either direction, the results would be the same.

"The way I saw it, we would have enough wood for burning to last us forever. Fish and game were abundant and even with the railroad coming through here I didn't expect that to change.

"Turning our mounts toward the west, I pointed out, 'You wanted to see mountains. While these may not be exactly like the ones you've seen in western paintings, those off in the distance are some powerful tall mountains! Tom told me those mountains manage to keep snow on their tops mostly year round.

Turning they rode back over to where Tom's cabin stood. Once again Thomas was standing in his garden area. 'I figured that was you coming back when I first laid eyes on the two of you,' Tipping his floppy hat in Darleen's direction, Tom said. 'So this is the Lady of the house. Glad to meet you!

'It's been quiet here since you left. I figure those Crow took whatever they took and thought they'd burned my place down to the ground so there was no reason for them coming back. I'm thinking they were just young bucks looking for bragging rights when they returned to their own people. I've a rifle in the cabin that they overlooked. I've got it pretty well hidden if I do say so myself. I carry this shotgun with me when I'm outdoors. If I shoot at something or someone, it won't kill them but this gun sure as Hell puts a load of buckshot in their hind-end that'll probably convince them to stay the Hell away!' Tom smiled after saying this. 'Forgive my language, Lady Darleen, most times I speak without really giving any regards to who is listening. And on top of that, you are the first female I've seen in over a year. You two actually thinking of setting up shop here along the Platte?'

'That's why we're both out here today. I told Darlene what I saw when I first checked this area out, and she wanted to see it for herself. We're running up against time so to speak. The wagon train we're traveling with will be leaving Fort Kearney in a few days. We've really got to make up our minds if we're going to settle here by the river or move on with the other wagons and settlers.' Simon said.

'Well you'll find as many, if not more, Indians the further west you go, and I'm led to believe they just get feistier with every mile you travel,' Tom said. 'Now as for the land here about, I honestly don't think you'll find better land anywhere between here and the ocean. Of course that's just my opinion.

'When I was much younger, I rode all the way out to Oregon just wanting to see the Pacific Ocean and do some trapping. Now the thing I remember most was the constant rain. Some of the Indians out that way were quite different from what we have here.

'The Shoshone were a good looking people, and I don't believe they have a bad bone in their body. They were the ones what helped Lewis and Clark back in eighteen and four. Come to think of it, Sacagawea, who they called "bird woman", was a Shoshone herself. Back then, I did a fair share of trapping. I might have settled out there with a good looking Shoshone woman if it wasn't for the awful rain and the wolves. Now this was all many years ago that I'm recalling.

'Today I figure I couldn't walk a mile if my life depended on it. And as for trapping, while I still have my traps, and there is more than enough game to be taken here about. But I doubt I could set a trap without getting my hand caught up in it. I just don't have the ability or the strength anymore.'

'Well maybe if we do decide to settle here,' Simon said, 'you'll be kind enough to teach me how to trap.'

'While I can't do it anymore,' Tom lamented, 'I'd be glad, more than glad, to pass on to you some trapping tricks I've used over the years. And I've still got my full basket of traps looking like the first day I bought them. That reminds me of another reason I left Oregon. Rain and metal just don't go together. In all my years of trapping, I always boiled my traps before I began my season. But out in Oregon, I found I couldn't get a full month out of my traps before I had to boil them once again and sometimes even had to coat the springs and trigger with oil which just made them useless. Animals are smart. A touch of oil or human scent on a trap, and no animal would come within a hundred feet of it.'

'Well I think Darlene and I should be starting back to

the fort. I also suspect that after we talk about what she has seen and heard here today, that we'll be returning and homesteading as your neighbor,' Simon said. Both shaking hands with Tom, Simon and Darlene mounted their horses and started back toward Fort Kearney.

"The next day found us back at the fort and after checking in on little Simon, Darleen and I sought out Roger and the wagon train group. Roger greeted us by asking what our decision was for staying or leaving with the wagon train."

'A rider came through about one hour ago and told us the stage would be here first thing tomorrow,' Roger said. 'If that turns out to be true, I'll be planning on pulling out of here the following morning at first light. I'm glad to see you back. What did Darlene think of the area you're looking at?'

'I do believe we'll be staying behind and homesteading on the land we've looked at,' Simon answered. 'I'm sure we'll talk more tonight, but I do believe we'll be staying right here by the fort for a few days in order to stock up and get ourselves organized. I'll be giving Paul a list of the lumber we'd like to have purchased at Omaha, and have delivered at our new site once the railroad extends that far. Paul will be ordering lumber for himself and the Union Pacific, so it should work out real well all the way around.

'Depending on the length of time it'll take getting the

finished lumber, we figure we can live out of our wagon. That will be no different than if we were still on the trail, plus I can be clearing our land in the meantime. Although it may be too late to get a crop in, I figure we can down enough meat to carry us through the coming winter.'

That night Simon, Darlene and their son ate with Martha, her husband James, and Sheri. Martha was sad to learn they would be leaving Simon, Darlene and the boy behind when the wagon train moved on. 'James has his heart set on settling in Cheyenne, Wyoming knowing he has friends already there.' Martha said.

'But you mark my words,' James said. "If Cheyenne doesn't pan out, we'll be headed right back here and finding a place near where you'll be living.'

Martha leaned over and put her hand on Darlene's arm. 'Who on God's green earth would have ever thought you and I would have established a bond such as we now share? I'm thinking back to Pemberton and feeling it was all just a dream, and a bad dream at that. I'm much happier with the way it is with you and me today,' she said.

"Mid-morning of the following day the stage arrived at the fort. There were letters from friends back home for just about every family on the wagon train. I got a letter from Richard Jarvis at Colt saying he was waiting to hear exactly where I would be settling down. As this was the very end of the line for the stage company, I had spent the previous night having Darlene write a letter to Richard telling him where and why we would be homesteading along the Platte River in Nebraska.

"We wrote of how the Union Pacific was now less than ten miles from where we would be filing a claim on our land. We hoped that by the coming spring, the railroad should be passing our location and also be building a depot and train station there. We believed a good-sized town would be built nearby within a year or two at most. I figured business would be slow at first, but that settlement of the area had already taken place by one group of who had already established themselves just north of Fort Kearney. I gave the letter to the stage driver to take back to St. Louis and forward it to Hartford from there.

"Roger was like a mother hen that final day before planning to head out. He walked from wagon to wagon pointing out wheels he believed needed greasing, and on one wagon, a wheel needed replacing. Canvas that needed patching, he brought to the owner's attention. Harness leather on several wagons needed attention or replacing also. Taking a rifle or pistol from each wagon owner, he ejected the shells while chatting with the owner. Over half the bullets ejected were green in color."

'These bullets haven't seen the light of day since you first put them in the gun,' Roger said. 'I expected to see shinny copper shells, instead I'm looking at the equivalent of green mold. I can only imagine what the inside of the barrel must look like. Before you do anything, I'm telling you to buy a box or two of new bullets. Then spend however long it takes to get this barrel spotless inside. Your life, and the life of your family, and even your friends on this wagon train, just might be counting on this weapon as we go forward.'

Reaching the end of the wagons, Roger crossed over and started up the other side. Stopping at each horse he gave the animal a thorough going over. Two were found needing new shoes. He suspected another one to be hurting, possibly from arthritis. 'I'd advise you look into replacing this horse before we start out,' he said. 'I don't believe it will last a full month before it will need to be put down.'

Calling the group together, Roger announced he was extending their leaving by one more day. 'I've seen a lot that needs attending to before we consider moving on. So we'll be starting west at sun-up the day after tomorrow. I've explained what I've seen as needing your attention. You've everything you need right here at the fort. I'm giving you another day and these extra hours to put everything in order. When you believe you are finished, ask me and I'll inspect what you've done. Work together and help each other.'

Three men approached Simon asking to purchase new pistols and new boxes of ammunition. 'These pistols and boxes of ammo are not mine. If they were, I'd gladly give them to you. But they belong to Colt Firearms in Hartford, Connecticut, and I have to account and pay for each and every item I sell. I will sell each one of you a new, in the box, Colt pistol, along with a full factory box of ammo for twenty-five dollars.' Simon said.

All three men thanked him for his offer and each bought a pistol along with a box of bullets. The blacksmith at the fort was kept busy shoeing horses along with cutting new leather that would replace worn out harnesses. Throughout the day wheels were greased and canvas was patched.

Captain Turner came out of the fort and walked alongside Roger until they came to the front wagon. 'I know you've told everyone you'd be leaving, but I'm asking you to reconsider. Not knowing how it is with regards to Iron Hand, I'd hate to see you out on the trail having to fight off an attack when you all could be safely waiting right here at the fort until we learn how Iron Hand is. We're also getting late in the season, so I know time is precious to you. All things considered, all I can do is ask.' The Captain said.

'If it's not Crow, then I suspect we'll be dealing with Sioux, Cheyenne, Dakota or even Pawnee as we head out.' Roger said. 'But I do see the smart thing is to wait at least until we learn if Iron Hand lives or dies.'

Roger looked up at the sky and then at the leaves on the nearby trees. 'Winter weather isn't that far off. If I was to hold up here for another week or so, it just might make it too late to attempt going further west till spring sets in. Then again I know you're right with regards to us at least knowing more about Iron Hand. It'll be close for sure, but I'll give it one more week staying put right here. I'll tell the people tonight and we'll see how that goes over with them. One more week Mark, then if we've heard nothing more, I figure I've no choice but to start west.'

'Well for better or worse,' Simon said, 'we have a bit of a breather with Roger staying here. I'll take our lumber list out to Paul, and while I'm there, I'll look into what we have to do in order to file a claim with the state and see what and how we pay the Union Pacific for the land we're intending to homestead. I figure I'll be back by mid-afternoon. We'll move out to the site we've decided on as soon as I get back. I'm hoping we finally hear something about Iron Hand and if he is alive or dead, but either way it is not going to change our plans.'

That day passed so quickly. The following day, Simon and family left Fort Kearney and started toward their chosen site along the Platte River. After two days of travel, they arrived at their homestead location in the early evening. Simon brought the wagon to a stop and unhitched the horses. Setting the brake on the wagon, he also placed a decent-sized rock against the front and rear of the two front wheels. 'Well, where do you figure we'll locate our house and in which direction do you want it facing?' he asked Darlene.

Darlene walked around for about five minutes before she spoke. 'We really should build our home facing the Platte,' she said. 'And the land over to the left appears to be perfect for clearing and setting out our garden.'

'Well, we'll be living out of the wagon until the lumber arrives,' Simon said. 'Tomorrow I'll be cutting down trees that I can make poles out of for securing the garden area. It looks fairly level where you want the house built, but we'll run a string or two just to make sure. Any high spots we see, we'll just knock them down.

'I hope we can get a stone foundation laid out before our lumber arrives. That will keep the house up off the ground. I can see many things needing doing before we'll feel secure here. Just clearing the garden and house area alone will take at least three weeks, and I doubt we'll get much of a crop in, if anything, considering the planting season is really at its end.'

That evening, they all three walked over to say hello to Tom. 'Well I'd say you've now planted your flag here for certain sure,' Tom said. 'I'm happy to be having you as a neighbor. I haven't seen an Indian around here since the first time you were here. But yesterday there were ten or twelve elk standing right about where you've set your wagon. I was tempted to shoot one, but the thought of all the work involved gutting and dressing it out, then quartering it and dragging it all the way over here, well I figured I've got enough meat set aside already to last me a month or two. Plus those critters won't be going very far away anytime soon.'

The following morning Simon and Darlene began clearing the planned garden area. Later in the day Simon walked over to visit with Tom. 'The Platte will freeze in certain spots during the winter, yet most of the river will continue to flow freely. That's when you can chop out blocks of Ice,' Tom told Simon. 'But it'll get cold enough here so you really won't be needing anything special to keep the ice in. And even as cold as it gets, I suspect you'll all be comfortable snuggled down inside your wagon at night.

'I see you've been cutting up some firewood. Now I'm not telling you what you ought to do, mind you, but if it were me, I'd cut and split some firewood every day. You'll be finding out that winter here seems to go on forever. I'd advise you stack up at least two cord of firewood before the snow starts. I always cut a top layer a good foot longer than my firewood. Snow will pile up on those top slabs allowing the wood stacked below to remain dry.

'Any animals you shoot, you'll find their hides excellent for clothing. When I kill any animal, I make sure nothing goes to waste. The hide becomes winter clothing, and the meat I eat. The tendons I cure and save, and I even crush up the bones and spread them in the garden area. They add a richness to the soil which is a good fertilizer. Antlers make fine handles for knives and such, and they sell well to settlers and people just passing through. All this I've no doubt you'll figure out yourself in time. And don't just be thinking of big animals. There is not much that's tastier than rabbit and squirrel. And again, their hide comes in awful handy for many uses.

'When I was younger and just starting out on my own, I'd find a sutler somewhere close, and I'd buy things there three, maybe four, times a year. I'm thinking I haven't bought anything from anyone now in a good ten years. I remember I was looking to buy an axe a few years back. Would have bought one too if I hadn't come across an abandoned wagon where I managed to get myself an axe, a shovel, and about a five by six foot piece of decent canvas. Both hind wheels were gone, so I figured whoever left that wagon, wasn't coming back.' .

Looking past Tom, Simon saw six mounted soldiers approaching. Coming to a halt opposite where Simon and Tom stood, the Sergeant leading this group dispatched two of his men to cross over and stay by Simon's wagon where he could see Darlene and her son standing.

The Sergeant saluted the two men and reported, 'Captain Turner sent this patrol out to inform you that Iron Hand has died. The Captain has offered any, who care to, may report to the fort to insure their safety. He'll give you a full report on what to expect, but I will tell you that these next couple of weeks could prove dangerous for settlers. Work on the railroad has stopped until Paul Atkins is satisfied enough with the situation that he is willing to put his workers once again back outside the Union Pacific's compound.'

'How do you see what's happening, Sergeant," Simon asked.

'The Crow will be choosing a new chief shortly. Other than for what I've just told you, I'll leave it up to Captain Turner to say anything more. I do believe you've a day, maybe two, before anything happens. But if it was me, and I had my family out here, I'd start for the fort as soon as possible.

'My orders are to advise the settlers at Dobytown, so that is where my patrol will be going from here. As for my men and myself, I fully intend on being back within the walls of Fort Kearney sometime tomorrow at the latest.' Signaling his men to join him, the patrol moved off at a gallop.

'Well, I'm staying right here.' Tom said. 'This cabin and my little garden are all I have. You're in a different situation having a family with you. Personally, if I were you, I'd heed the Sergeant's advice and hightail it back to Fort Kearney. Everything might just blow over in a few days. The way I see it, it's anybody's guess, but better safe than sorry I've always heard.'

Simon crossed over to his family and related to Darlene

what the Sergeant had told him. 'I say we pack up and head to the fort,' Darlene said. 'Once we learn what is happening with the Crow Indians, then we can decide if and when it's time to come back here.'

'I've no problem with that,' Simon said. 'Captain Turner wouldn't have sent a patrol out here if he wasn't worried himself. I'll hitch up the horses while you gather up anything we've got laying around outside. Once we're ready to roll, I'll check the rifle and pistol just to be on the safe side. I wish I could get Tom to come along with us, but his feet are planted firm. There is no way he'll consider leaving.' Within the hour, Simon and family were starting for the fort.

'The Crow will be choosing a new chief to replace Iron Hand.' Captain Mark Turner said as Simon and Roger sat down with him. 'From what I'm hearing it's a choice between a somewhat decent feller, and a real firebrand. Now Iron Hand was somewhere in between these two so to speak. He leaned more to the feisty side, and was more than a bit of a bluffer and a thief. But there were times when I came close to arresting him. The only thing stopping me was lack of evidence. I knew in my heart he'd killed settlers and burned wagons and cabins. But I just couldn't prove it.

'And as for stealing, I honestly believe he thought it a poor day when he didn't steal something from someone. Hell, he tried to walk out of this very fort with a canvas tarp that he swore he'd paid for. We had a tense moment or two, I can tell you. His Indians formed up just outside the gate, and my men in formation at attack mode along the walls facing off with each other.

'He finally threw the tarp on the ground just inside the gate and mounted his pony. His warriors had their bows and rifles out, and my men had their rifles out pointing at them also. That was the longest two minutes I can ever remember. Finally he waved at his warriors, turned his horse around, stood up in his saddle and showed me his backside, then they all rode off away from this fort.

'The better of the two choices, as far as I'm concerned, is called White Feather. I've met him a couple of times, and he always seemed to me to be reasonable.' Mark said. 'The other one I understand is known as Raven. I also have been told his soul is as black as his name. I'm thinking if Raven is chosen to replace Iron Hand as chief, we'll have some serious fighting on our hands in short order. He'll be out to make a name for himself, and whatever he does he'll act quickly. I've already had an offer from Fort Seward of a full company of cavalry if Raven is chosen. But meanwhile, until we learn more, I want you to drive your wagon inside this fort', the Captain said while pointing at Simon.

'I've a small storeroom that I've had the men empty. I'd appreciate it if you and your family would take up residence there until we know exactly what we'll be up against. I'd also deeply appreciate it if you would store your pistols and ammo there. I hate to think of them laying in your wagon out where you're setting up a homestead. They will be much safer in that room and you'll have access to them whenever you desire to check on them.'

Three days later, four wagons came into view with their horses lathered and running at a full gallop. 'Corporal of the guard,' the sentry called out. 'Advise the Captain, we have settlers' wagons coming to the fort! Bugler, sound the alarm and turn out the troops, this looks like trouble to me!'

The wagons stopped right at the front gate and civilians immediately jumped out of them running to enter the fort. Arrows could be seen stuck in each of the wagons, and a lady that had been sitting beside the driver of the first wagon was slumped over with two arrows embedded in her back. 'We've more injured inside these wagons!' The driver yelled to the soldiers.

'Who is the wagon master?" Captain Turner asked as he ran past the open gate and stopped beside the first wagon.

'Jeff Thornton was guiding us civilians,' a man on the second wagon answered. 'He's laying back on the trail where this all started earlier this morning. The Indians came at us, and Jeff was the first to be killed. I believe he was scalped, also. There were at least thirty Indians, and arrows were flying everywhere. I'd say two or three settlers were hit before any of us fired off our first shot.'

'Stop right there,' Captain Turner said to the man speaking, 'Let's get these folks taken care of first. You soldiers gather up the wounded and get them in to see the doctor. I also want these horses unhitched from the wagons, and the wagons set off to the side of the fort. Bring the horses inside and detail men to rub them down, and check them for any injuries they may have suffered. Any of the dead found in the wagons, I want taken into the fort also.'

'What about the children them Indians carried off?' another man shouted. 'And there are still two wagons left behind when we decided to make a run for it.'

'I'll sort it all out as quickly as I can, and then I'll send a patrol out to see about the wagons left behind.' The Captain said as he turned and walked back into the fort with the driver of the second wagon walking beside him. 'And your name is?' Turner asked.

'Hudak, Sir! Jack Hudak, from Ohio,' he said. 'They hit us minutes after we'd gotten our wagons into line and were starting for the fort.' Jack told the Captain. 'Jeff told us we'd be arriving here at this fort sometime late this afternoon. We hadn't gone but a half mile when we heard their war cry and suddenly they were all around us. Arrows were flying in the air, and those in our group that were walking, began running to catch up to their wagons.

'I guess there were a half dozen young children walking when this began, I saw a couple of Indians swoop down and each picked up a child. Others tell me that all together, three children were captured and taken away. Now you tell me why in heaven's name they would steal away the children?

'Anyhow after I saw Jeff topple off his horse and a couple of Indians run to him, I have to believe they scalped him. I hollered at Frank who was driving the first wagon, to use his whip on the horses and get us the Hell out of there. The Indians cut off the back two wagons, and I suspect they killed the drivers, if not the people in the wagons also. But I honestly didn't look back to see. The Indians chased us for less than half a mile and then just stopped, turned around, and rode back to the two wagons they'd captured.'

'Sounds to me like Raven won the vote to become Chief.' Captain Turner said, shaking his head. 'Corporal of the guard,' Turner hollered. 'Have Sergeant Riley mount forty men and return to the scene where this all happened to see what he can learn. Tell him to report back directly to me. Tell him to be thorough, but that I want him and his men to be back inside this fort as soon as possible. I don't want him following any Indians or any trail they may have left. Learn all he can at the scene and return to the fort as ordered.'

The Corporal entered the Captain's office and began to

speak when Captain Turner cut him off sharply. Turning to Jack Hudak, he thanked him for his patience and information. 'Go back to your family Jack. I'll call on you again if need be. Meanwhile, I thank God you and yours are safe inside this fort now.'

After Jack left the office, Mark leaned forward and explained to the Corporal, that he suspected whatever the Corporal was about to say, there was no need for a civilian to be hearing it.

Standing at attention, the Corporal reported, 'Sergeant Riley left the fort not ten minutes ago as ordered. So far the dead civilians we have at the moment amount to five. Several people have confirmed that three children were taken alive by the Indians during the attack. All the horses from the wagon train seem to be in decent shape. Private Jackson is feeding and watering them now. Several arrows pulled from the wagons are Crow arrows.'

'Thank you Corporal, please see to it that these civilians are made as comfortable as possible. Pass the word among these settlers that I'll be talking to each and every one of them before this day is done.'

'Sir,' the Corporal asked. 'I've always believed this was Pawnee country. How is it we're now dealing with Crow Indians?'

'This is Pawnee country, let there be no doubt about that,

but most Indian tribes are nomads. They may claim one place as their home and another as their hunting or trapping ground. The strongest rule the roost. Tomorrow it might be the Sioux that push onto Pawnee-claimed land. If so, it'll be up to the Crow to fight or leave. But for now I have my hands full with Crow Indians. Crow Indians that have attacked and massacred innocent civilians. They will pay a terrible price for what they have done, I assure you as I shall assure these civilians involved! We'll wait for the report from the patrol and learn what they have discovered, if anything. Then, and only then, I'll make my decision.' Captain Turner promised.

Later as the Captain walked among the civilians, stopping and chatting with each huddled group, he made it perfectly clear that he would get the stolen children back and get them back soon. 'Tomorrow we'll bury the dead. It'll be done respectfully and with God's blessing.'

"Later his patrol returned to the fort. They brought back four bodies they had recovered at the scene. The two wagons were gone, and these bodies had been scalped and then dumped at the side of the trail. They found no children!

"Early the following morning, the Captain mounted his horse and led one hundred cavalry out of the fort. With them were two cannon each being drawn by a caisson with six soldiers assigned to each cannon. Riding northeast at a gallop, they came within sight of the Crow camp six hours later. At a walk, Captain Turner brought his cavalry within shouting distance of the Crow camp. Off to his right stood the two wagons these Indians had captured the day before. Freeing the cannon from their limbers, both were turned facing the Indian camp. Quickly both cannons were loaded and made ready to fire. Indians could be seen gathering together, when suddenly Raven mounted his horse and slowly approached the soldiers."

'Go from this place,' he shouted at the soldiers. 'This is Crow land now, and I am, Raven, Chief of these people.'

Captain Turner leaned forward in his saddle and said, 'Raven, call forward the men who rode with you yesterday and attacked the settler's wagons. I also command you to bring forward the three white children your people have taken.'

'Again I tell you, take your soldiers and go from this place! You have no right here." Raven commanded.

'What you see before you, I have also placed behind your village.' Mark bluffed. 'I'll only ask once more, bring out the white children you have taken, and call those who rode with you yesterday to come forward.'

'And for the last time,' Raven said, 'go! So my people will not have to look upon you.'

With a nod of his head, Captain Mark Turner indicated the nearest gun to fire. When the men fired the cannon, shot ripped through the village. Several Indians were hit, while two teepees were destroyed. When the sound of the shot ceased, Captain Turner told Raven to get down from his horse and kneel upon the ground. 'Now before you, and you alone, force me to completely wipe out this village, I'll ask once again, have your warriors bring out the white children, now!'

Reluctantly, Raven waved his hand toward his people. Two warriors brought out the three white children who quickly ran forward toward the soldiers. 'You have done an honorable thing. Now call for those who rode with you yesterday to come forward and kneel with you.' The Captain said.

'You have me! That is enough.' Raven said.

With another nod to his gunners, the second cannon fired at the village. Once again over a hundred canister balls flew throughout the village. This time three teepees were knocked to the ground and several Indians were either killed or injured.

'You do not understand, Raven, it is I who command here, not you. Now call out those who rode with you yesterday.'

Hollering to his people, six warriors came forward and stood by Raven.

'This is but a small number of warriors who followed you and massacred innocent civilians and stole their children.' Mark noted. 'Yes, it is but a small number of those who followed you. But it will have to do. I will let the other warriors that rode with you continue to live among their people in shame.' Ordering several of his men to dismount, he directed them to tie the Indians' hands together, then to tie an additional rope linking the Indians together.

'You will pay for this insult!' Raven threatened.

'Yes, I will pay for what I do here today, but not in the way you think I will pay. And you will not be alive to see me pay.' Turning to his soldiers who held the rope tied to the Indians, he ordered them to have the Indians kick off their moccasins before they started their walk back to the fort, forcing the group of Indians to walk barefoot behind the soldiers.

'Retrieve the two wagons these vermin have stolen,' he ordered his remaining men. Ride into the village and locate the horses for these wagons. Then have the Indians do the work of hitching the horses to the wagons.'

Riding forward alone, he entered the Crow village. From his mount, he addressed the rest of the tribe, 'If the Crow attack another wagon train or even just a lone settler, I will return and wipe this village and all of its people from the face of the Earth.

'You will find only the moccasins of the men I have taken back to the fort. These men will answer for the terrible thing they have done! Let their empty moccasins be a reminder to the Crow people. Choose your next leader wisely.'

"Late that afternoon Captain Mark Turner returned to the fort with his soldiers. That evening Raven and the six Crow Indians who had been brought to the fort were made to stand below the observation blockhouse at the corner of the fort. The civilians who had suffered the attack were asked if these were the Indians who had attacked them and stole the children. Raven was really the only one they could positively identify.

"Captain Turner thanked them, then requested they return to their wagons. Two hanging ropes were passed down from the tower, and soldiers set the loops around the necks of two of the Crow Indians. Quickly they were lifted up off the ground with their feet kicking at the air. When they were dead, two more were dispatched in the same way. And so it was with the last two.

"Raven had been made to watch each of his warriors hung. Then it was his turn. Before he was hung, Captain Turner told him that unlike his warriors, he would be left to hang against the wall of the fort for three days, while the other six would be taken out and thrown into a ditch beside where they had attacked the civilians."

'After three days, your body will be taken into the woods and burned. I will see to it that there shall be nothing of you left to sit before the "Great Counsel" who you believe is waiting for you in your next life. There will be nothing of you left but ashes that will be scattered by the winds!'

"Damn!" shouted Simon as he wiped his eyes of free-flowing tears. "Look at me crying like a baby! I do apologize, Miss Jessie, but every time I think of what those poor settlers went through, I tear up.

"Do you think we could end for the day? I know I said I wanted to finish today but I sure am exhausted from my emotions. How about we go for a walk in the Lexington Park just down the street? It's only 2:00 now and we could finish up tomorrow."

"Why, that sounds fine with me, Simon. I haven't been there in awhile and I like to check out the gardens in the park this time of year. I especially like to check out the native wildflowers and prairie plants. Let's go see how many we recognize! I think we both need a break!"

Chapter 10
Simon's World Turns Upside Down

"**G**ood morning, Simon. I hope you rested well last night. Are you ready to begin?" asked Jessie as she adjusted her notebook and settled her glasses. "I believe we left off with Raven's demise."

The following morning I approached Captain Turner and asked, 'What do you think will happen now?'

'Think?' Mark said. 'I know what will happen. Washington will get my report and I'll be relieved from duty. A good soldier can't go hanging Indians that have surrendered without a proper trial. It makes for bad press, although it does sell dime store novels that the people back east can't seem to get enough of.

'During the war I was a full Colonel. Two months after the war ended, I was a civilian once again. Then with the help of friends I had in Washington, I was appointed Captain and given this fort as my assignment. Another year and I believe I'd have made Major and been ready to retire. But that all ended yesterday.

'No, my friend, I don't have to think one little bit about what will happen. And to tell you the truth, I have no regrets. Those in Washington will do far worse to the Native Indian than what I did yesterday. But they'll do their work quietly, and behind closed doors.'

"A few days later, my family and I left Fort Kearney and rode out to our homestead site. Tom was fine, and anxious to hear what had happened since the soldiers were last at his place."

'Well,' Simon began, 'Our going back to the fort was a real smart move. It seems Raven won out and became Chief. He didn't waste any time showing his hand. He attacked a wagon train and killed about ten people. His warriors also took three white children captive. Within twenty-four hours, Captain Turner took one hundred men and two cannon out to the Crow village. He captured Raven along with six of his warriors. I hear he also fired both cannons into the village when Raven and the Crow didn't obey his orders as quickly as he wanted. He recovered the three children and both of the stolen wagons. Mark made the Indians walk all the way back to the fort barefoot.

'After the settlers who'd been attacked pointed out Raven, Mark hung all seven of the Indians. Six of them, he had some soldiers take their bodies out to where the attack on the wagon train took place. I'm told they dumped these bodies in a ditch beside the site. As for Raven, before he was hung, Mark told him he would hang there at the fort for three days. Then his body would be taken into the woods and burned until there was nothing left of it but ashes.'

Tom looked all around and then wiped his forehead before speaking. 'Seems to me we'll be dealing with these Indians for a while yet. Today it is the Crow, I suspect tomorrow it'll be Sioux or possibly Cheyenne. Can't say as I really blame them. This was their land after all. I just wish there was a way clear for all of us, Indian and settlers alike, to share the land and live peacefully side by side.

'I remember in the treaty at Laramie in 1868, the Indians were promised this land for as long as the grass grew and the waters flowed. But I guess words are just words to some people, and what's said today isn't necessarily true tomorrow. These Crow shouldn't even be here, they belong back northwest on the land they claim to own.'

Simon crossed back over onto his homestead and picked up his son. Darlene looked up at the sky and slowly shook her head and stated, 'Seems to me we've a long winter coming.'

"The civilians who'd been attacked decided to spend the

winter at Fort Kearney, unless Roger was willing to take them along with his group. None of them really wanted to stay at the fort with all the memories it held. Roger spoke with each group of settlers and it was decided all but one family would join his group and continue west. Two of the children that had been captured by the Crow were now orphans. The husband and wife who chose to remain at the fort took these children under their protection."

'I'm Walter Fitzgerald. My wife, Peggy, and I figure we'll stay right here through the winter and decide come spring if we want to go on, settle here somewhere close by, or return to New York. No matter what, these two girls will never want for anything as long as Peggy and I are alive. Their folks lived near us in New York. We've known them since before these girls were born. We all had such plans for our future out west. Now I'm thinking that come springtime we'll see to it that we're a regular family.'

Two days later Roger started his wagon train west once again. Mark ordered Raven's body cut down and taken into the woods to be burned. Simon had spoken with Paul at the Union Pacific compound and managed to get five empty crates that equipment had been shipped in. These he carefully broke down for the lumber, and at his site, he erected a small affair to keep his horses in over the coming winter while protecting them from the weather.

The second week at the site, Simon shot an elk. Tom gave him a hand butchering the animal. 'I wish you'd have waited another week or two,' Tom said. 'I do think by then we'd have enough snow on the ground that would make moving this brute a little easier. But it's cold enough now that you won't have to bother salting the meat. I'm thinking Mother Nature will freeze it good and proper in no time at all.' That evening Tom ate elk steaks with his new neighbors beside their wagon. The following day the snow began to fall at noon. It snowed for three straight days, leaving Simon's family and Tom with two feet of fresh snow. On that third day the temp dropped to five degrees. Winter had begun.

In February the snow was four feet on the level at Simon's homestead site. On the tenth of the month, Darlene awoke to see six Pawnee Indians on horses just twenty yards from the wagon. Quickly she woke Simon who dressed and climbed outside. One Indian walked his horse forward, stopping within ten feet of Simon. Repeatedly putting his hand to his mouth, he indicated he and those with him were hungry. Darlene came out of the wagon and stood beside Simon.

Seeing these Indian's needs, she quickly had Simon start a fire in the fire pit that they kept covered from falling snow. Reaching into the wagon, Darlene brought out a large cast iron frying pan, along with a package of meat. Within minutes the food was cooking and the Indians dismounted and approached the fire to warm themselves.

By waving their hands and pointing off to the northwest, they indicated they had come from a distance far away.

Before they ate, one warrior unbuckled a bear hide from his horse. This he spread on the snow near the fire pit. Then each Indian came forth and placed something upon this hide. One put a knife with a staghorn handle. Another laid down a beaded belt, and so it went until each Indian had given something to Simon and Darlene. After eating their fill, they raised their hands and clapped. Turning to walk back to their horses, Simon called for them to stop. Reaching down he picked up the knife from the Bear hide and handed it to one of the Indians. He then did the same with each item they had placed on the hide as a gift in return for the food. Picking up the bear hide, Simon draped it over Darlene's shoulders letting it fall and cover her back. Then he raised his hands and clapped also. Extending his hand to the first Indian that had approached him, he was pleased to see this man shake his hand.

Within minutes, the Indians were gone. For a moment Simon and Darlene thought this had all been a dream, but the fire still burned, the cast iron skillet needed cleaning, and Darlene reached behind her and pulled the bear hide tightly against her back.

Later Tom came over to talk with them. 'I was awake and saw them Indians ride almost up to your wagon. I had my shotgun ready, and at the first sign of trouble, I figured to draw their attention to me and away from you two and the boy.

'They appeared to be Pawnee. But it was the damnedest thing I ever witnessed. I swear. Now you tell me if you can, why all Indians can't be like them. Reminded me of the Indians I met when I was younger and out further west.

'But it just goes to show that there are good and bad in both our people. Well, I guess I'll be dead and it will be up to you younger folk to figure it all out. I just know it doesn't have to go on the way it is now. Both sides have to learn to get along.'

When spring finally broke, Simon began clearing the area where they intended to plant their garden. As the days passed, they began to hear the work being done on the rails coming closer and closer. Day following day, Simon and his son brought rocks up from the river bed to construct a solid foundation for what would become their house. By April he'd turned the earth throughout the clearing where they would be planting their garden.

By May, Darlene had the garden planted. Young Simon stayed by his mother, helping with the garden whenever he wasn't working with his father. It was during this spring, young Simon was taught to handle and shoot one of the Colt pistols.

Finally, as the days grew warmer, the railroad crew came into view. They were a good mile north of the land Simon was homesteading. As things worked out, it was almost Fall when they settled on the area to locate the train station. This was a further half mile west.

In September, a flat car arrived with the lumber Simon had ordered. Paul assigned two men from the railroad to assist Simon getting the framing up on Simon's cabin. Two weeks later Simon and his son were up nailing boards that would become the roof. Paul stopped by on his way to the proposed station site to check on Simon's progress. Telling his son to take a break, Simon climbed down and shook hands with Paul.

'What do I owe you for the two men who helped me get the framing up?' Simon asked.

'Nothing,' Paul said. 'I hear you gave them a fine bottle of Virginia Whiskey for their effort. They are good roughin, and good finished carpenters. But I had no work or need for them until we start on building the train station. By the way, when my supplies for the station arrived, I came up with two extra windows. You're welcome to them if you think you can fit them into your cabin plans.'

'Darlene will be pleased as punch when she hears this,' Simon said. 'But I insist on paying you for the windows.'

'No can do,' Paul said. 'The Union Pacific has already

paid for everything, and the paperwork has long since cleared the main office. I'll tell you what, once we begin building the train depot, I'll stop by and have dinner with you and your family. That will relieve your conscience over the windows.'

By October the leaves on the trees were all gone. Most of the garden produce had been stored in barrels filled with river sand to keep them from spoiling. Simon had the cabin closed in with both windows facing out toward the Platte River. 'We'll make do living in our cabin, using blankets and things from the wagon. Over the winter I'll be making furniture,' he said.

'Not necessary,' Darlene answered. 'We can make do as you say until spring. But then with the train up and running, the boy and I can take the train back to Omaha, or even St. Louis, and purchase real factory-made furniture. Once I've purchased what we want, I'm sure with your connection with Paul, we'll be able to load everything on the train and bring it right back almost to our front door. And we've had a bountiful garden considering this is our first try at gardening,' Darlene said. 'I've enough greens along with potatoes and carrots, beets and sweetcorn, and the list just goes on and on. One thing we do need is salt. When winter comes and you go out trapping with Tom, be on the lookout for a site where we can harvest salt. Maybe Tom even knows of one.'

With the railroad and the new train depot, Lexington

had thrived. In one year over fifty houses were built alongside the Platte River. Paul straw-bossed the work for the Union Pacific, but always managed to add one or two boxcars or flatbed railcars onto trains coming out of Omaha. These were always loaded with finished lumber available to the settlers.

In partnership with Simon, the lumber was paid for in advance and sold at a minimal twenty-percent profit which they split evenly. Meanwhile, Simon's sale of Colt pistols progressed rapidly. Now Richard at Colt could ship his pistols and ammunition directly to Lexington via the Union Pacific Railroad.

'When I move on,' Paul said, 'you'll have to keep me informed of the lumber needs we'll have here. I'll handle everything as I push the tracks west. We'll raise our margin on the lumber we provide to twenty-five percent. This will give you fifteen percent, and I'll continue with my ten percent. The way I see it everyone - you, me and the settlers- all make out well. Eventually, I'll pick up more on my end the further west I go.'

As they were speaking, word came that George Armstrong Custer was reporting the discovery of gold in the Black Hills. Within days, those in Washington were busy planning on moving the Native Indians out of that area and opening the land to settlers. In eighteen seventy-four, Custer was taking his seventh cavalry into the Black Hills to explore and map the area. George

Armstrong Custer had nine hundred men with him, along with three Gatling guns. He also took some miners along to determine if there really was gold in the area. All this was in direct violation of the treaty of Laramie signed in eighteen sixty-eight.

'The Sioux won't stand still for this,' Tom said when Simon told him what he'd heard. 'I'm thinking the Indians have been pushed just about as far as they are going to allow them in Washington to keep breaking the treaties. My best guess is, if all the tribes get together, they will be able to push every settler and soldier all the way back to east of the Mississippi, even possibly back to Washington itself.'

Later talking with Darlene, Simon related what Tom had said, and the news he himself had been hearing. 'I'm torn between staying put, and wanting to pack our wagon up and leaving everything we have accomplished here and heading back east. What are you thinking?' she asked.

'I'm thinking that time moves on,' Simon said. 'Washington just fought a horrible Civil War against a united army that wanted to keep slavery and dissolve the Union. These tribes are not united, and I can't see them standing against the Union. There are as many, if not more, soldiers and settlers west of the Mississippi today than there are Indians.

'I suspect there will be fighting and maybe sometimes the Indians will win. But in the long run, their time has come and gone. The soldiers will gobble them up, one tribe after another. We're taking a gamble staying here, but it's a gamble I'm willing to take as long as you agree with me.

'Like I've just said, time moves on. Were we to go back east, I believe we'd face far worse than what we face staying here. There was a time right after the war that you and I living together was accepted back east. I don't believe that feeling remains as strong today. Maybe I'm wrong, but it's a gut feeling I have.'

'Well here we'll stay then,' Darlene said. 'I'll be praying any fighting that will be coming, will stay well north and west of us. Captain Turner has already set an example for the Indians locally. General Custer ought to leave the Black Hills immediately! He's only stirring the pot for his own good.

'Like you said, time moves on. Custer has had his day already, if he has his way, all he'll do now is make life miserable for the Indians and settlers alike. He won't be satisfied until he starts a war with the Indians, and to Hell with any concerns for us settlers. Custer is for Custer, and I truly believe he'll do anything including ball-faced-lying if it will get him in the limelight once again.'

"Within a month, Custer was proclaiming gold in the Black Hills. Within days, miners were entering the Black

Hills in violation of the US Government treaty. Despite the fact the miners were finding nothing in the way of gold, the flames continued to be fanned. By April of eighteen seventy-six, Custer had his war with the Sioux. By June twenty-fifth, eighteen seventy-six, Custer was facing Sioux, Cheyenne and Arapaho Indians at the battle of the Little Big Horn. In less than one hour, Custer, along with two hundred and ten of his command, would be dead.

"All that Darleen had predicted about Custer's need for fame came true. In September, Sioux along with Cheyenne warriors attacked Fort Kearney. Several soldiers caught outside the fort were massacred where they stood. Some braves left the fight at the fort to attack settlements in the area. With the exception of four survivors, Dobytown was wiped out. The shanty-type houses that had been built were all burned to the ground. Even the cut trees set aside by the settlers to be milled into useable lumber at a future date were set on fire.

"At Lexington a band of Cheyenne set fire to the railroad station after killing the two men assigned there. Tom was once again in his garden when the Cheyenne attacked. As several Indians set fire to his house, Tom fired his double barrel shot gun, killing two and wounding one other warrior. His shooting also alerted me to the attack underway.

"Six Cheyenne crossed over to our homestead only to be met with gunfire from little Simon and me. Darlene was standing in the garden when the attack began. Taking aim with her pistol, she fired at the closest Indian. When hit, this warrior turned his horse toward where Darlene stood just as she fired a second time. As the Indian slid from his mount and fell to the ground, another Indian took aim and fired at Darlene.

"Screaming and hollering to each other while dodging bullets coming from me and my son in the house, along with Tom having reloaded his shotgun for the third time, the small band of Indians fled the scene riding in the direction of Fort Kearney.

"As the Indian who had just shot at Darlene passed within thirty yards of Tom's garden at a full gallop, Tom took aim and fired both barrels of his shotgun. When hit this Indian fell from his horse seconds before his horse also went down.

"For several minutes no one moved. I told my son to lay on the floor, while I ran to check on Darlene. Tom came out of his garden and slowly approached the horse and Indian he'd shot. The Cheyenne lay face down in the pathway dead. The horse had been mortally injured. As Darlene and I joined Tom, Darlene leaned forward and shot, killing the wounded animal."

'We'll bury the horse and the dead Indians,' Darlene said. 'But before we do, I want every stich of clothing off these Indians. And I want the blanket off this horse also.' Having said this, Darlene fell to the ground. It was only then that Simon realized his Lady had actually been shot.

'Mama, Mama,' her child hollered as he ran out of the house toward his mother laying in the roadway. I grabbed my son and held him back, away from his mother.

'Easy child,' I said holding Little Simon. 'You run back to the house and get me a blanket and some water. I'll check Mother. I'm sure she'll be alright. Maybe we'll have to take her to Fort Kearney, to the doctor, but she'll be alright. Hurry, now, get me the water and a blanket.'

"Tom knelt beside Darlene and turned her ever so slowly in order to asses her wound. She was laying in a pool of blood, and her blouse appeared soaked with blood also. 'This looks mighty bad Simon,' Tom whispered looking up at me. 'Mighty bad I'm here to say, although I don't like saying it. You'd best be getting her to Fort Kearney and having the doctor there take a look see at her.'

"Kneeling, I felt for a pulse on Darlene's neck. It was there, but ever so slight. 'I'll hitch up your wagon,' Tom whispered. 'Send the boy to me the second he gets back with the water and blanket. I'm thinking there's no need for him to see his mother this way.'

"The following five minutes seemed to pass in slow motion. White puffy clouds were scattered across the sky, but a large cloud directly overhead was black across the length of its bottom half and blocked the sunlight that was just now overhead. Placing my hand on Darlene's shoulder, I began crying.

"Memories of her flooded my mind going back to our days at the Plantation in South Carolina. I remembered our first meeting in Providence, Rhode Island and later her giving birth to young Simon. As if in a dream, I saw her splashing in the water where we had camped in Pennsylvania as we were coming west."

'Hold on Darlene' I whispered to her, knowing this was not to be and feeling it deep inside. Turning my head I looked off away at the mountains in the distance. Ever so gently I turned her head in that direction. 'Look at your mountains, darling. Do you see the snow laying across them? You came to see the mountains, but there is so much more you told me you wanted to see.

'Stay with me. Our son needs us both. We've so much waiting ahead for us to experience, you must not go away, and I can't live without you.' When my son returned with a jug of water and a blanket, I sent him away immediately saying, 'Help Tom hitch up the wagon. We'll be taking Mother to the fort to see the doctor.'

"Before Tom finished hitching up the wagon, I felt once again for a pulse on Darlene's neck. This time her neck was cold and I could feel nothing. Fully laying down beside her now, I could see she had died. In seconds, my body was racked with my sobbing.

"Looking back over at me, Tom could read and understand the signs he was seeing. Dropping the bridle he held in his hand, he asked the boy to stay by the wagon. Reaching me, Tom knelt beside me and placed both hands on my back. 'I'll cry later' he said quietly and softly. 'You let it all out before the boy realizes what has happened. He'll be looking to you for guidance. Let the memories live, they will wipe away the pain in time.' He returned to our son to explain what happened."

"Oh, Simon, what a terrible thing to have happened!"

cried Jessie as she went to Simon and held him until his tears subsided.

That night Simon sat beside a fire pit he'd made many weeks before. This night a bright fire blazed between the rocks. Young Simon lay on a blanket at his side. Although he was sound asleep, the boy had his hand draped over his father's leg. It would be many a week before he'd sleep without his hand touching his father.

'Security,' Tom had said when he first witnessed it. 'Good for the boy and good for you,' Tom had added.

"For almost two weeks I did little or nothing. Thoughts constantly raced through my mind regarding just what I would do now that Darlene was gone. I buried my Lady in a forested glen a mile from the homestead. Standing at her grave, I could see both the snowcapped mountains to the north and the Platte River down behind their homestead. Soon after setting down roots in Lexington, Darleen and I had time to explore the general area. Here, just north of our property, Darlene had marveled when coming upon a large patch of goldenrod.

'They say Goldenrod is a weed, an herb and a wildflower,' Darleen exclaimed. 'Isn't it just beautiful? Damn! But it is so me! I swear I could stay here forever.' Looking up at the mountains and back at the green glen with its goldenrod, she said 'If ever Lexington gets too crowded, let's think about moving out here.'

"Two weeks to the day, a cavalry officer from Fort Kearney, leading an eight-man troop, arrived at our homestead."

'Captain Turner's Compliments,' the lieutenant said as he brought his mount to a halt. 'The Captain extends his apologies for our delay in getting out here. Two weeks back we had an attack at Fort Kearney. Dobytown was wiped out in that Indian attack. Plus we lost a few men at the fort before the Indians were finally beaten off. I see your house is still standing. Have you seen, or had any problem with the Indians?'

Simon bowed his head and spoke as if talking to the ground. 'We killed a few a couple of weeks back. I buried my Lady the day after the attack. My neighbor along with my son helped in fighting them. I buried four Cheyenne we'd killed before we'd run the others off. I buried them together in a grave I dug halfway down toward the train depot.' Simon raised his head and looked directly at the lieutenant.

'You say Dobytown was wiped out?' Saying this Simon's tears began again. The lieutenant climbed down from his horse and approaching Simon, put his gloved hand upon Simon's shoulder.

'I'm sorry sir,' the lieutenant said. 'Sorry for your loss and having to tell you about the settlers over at Dobytown. I'm thinking you must have known some of those people.'

'I'd met a few when I first arrived here. They were decent people, no need for them to have been killed.' Simon said.

'I'll make a report when I return to Fort Kearney, but I'm sure the Captain would like you to stop at the fort and give him a full first-hand report on what happened here.'

'I may get to the fort sometime tomorrow or maybe the following day,' Simon said. 'I'll be bringing my boy with me. Can't see leaving him here not knowing what's coming next. I've got a good neighbor just across the wagon path there. I hate leaving him if I'm just going to the fort. But Tom's set in his ways and I really can't see even trying to get him to go along with us when we head out.

'Then again, I will offer him the chance to go to the fort with us. Maybe he can add something about what happened here to what I'll be telling the Captain. You just might ride over and encourage him to go with me when I head out.' For the rest of the day Simon wondered from one thing to another without any real purpose. There was a large hole in his world and he hadn't yet even begun to fill it.

Later Tom crossed over and lit a fire in the circular stone pit. 'Thought I'd cook us up a mess of trout for the boy's supper. There's enough here for all three of us if you're hungry,' Tom said. 'I also brought a few elk steaks in case fish doesn't tickle your fancy. I know I should eat. The boy ought to be eating also, and it wouldn't hurt none if you put something in your gut beside just grief. But you suit yourself, I'll pretend I understand.'

Simon picked at a trout and watched his son eating. Young Simon used a knife like his father had shown him months earlier. Placing the blade against one side of the trout, he leaned the blade over so it resulted in a thin cut. With one stroke he moved the knife blade down along the backbone to the tail of the trout. Pushing the flesh onto his plate, he turned the fish over and repeated this movement on the opposite side. One piece was all that remained when he'd laid the knife down. All that remained was the head of the trout along with the complete attached boned skeleton. 'Mom would have wanted this for the garden,' the boy said, 'should I keep it or toss in in the fire?' he asked his father.

'Set it aside.' his father answered softly while rubbing the boy's head and hair. 'Waste not, want not, we'll decide later.' Simon looked over at Tom as he spoke. 'Tomorrow, or the day after, I figure to go to Fort Kearney and tell Captain Turner what happened here. I'm guessing I'll learn something more about Dobytown and what happened at the fort also. Maybe you could come along with the boy and me. I'm sure the Captain would be interested in hearing what you saw happen here.'

'That soldier asked me to talk to the Captain when he was here. I guess I could go along with you. It's been a few years since I was at the fort. I've a few skins I've tanned that are taking up space over at my place. Maybe I'll haul them along and have a look see at what the Sutler will be interested in paying for them.' Tom said. Two days later Simon, his son and Tom started for Fort Kearney seated on Simon's Conestoga wagon.

Five settlers from Dobytown greeted Simon when he arrived at the fort. Bert Webster was one of the survivors of the massacre that had taken place there. 'Weren't no reason or sense for what happened,' Bert said. 'The settlers killed had dealt with Crow, Cheyenne, Arapaho and I don't know how many different Indians in the few years they'd been settled at Dobytown. Never had a lick of problems dealing with the Natives.

'The truth be known, off and on there had been a fair amount of trading taking place. I lay it all on Custer. To those back East, he will no doubt end up a hero in most people's eyes. But to those of us out here who experienced what happened and believe why it happened, he'll always be a scoundrel of the first order.'

Simon and Tom both told Captain Turner what had happened when they were attacked. Thanking Tom, then asking Simon to stay with him awhile, he nodded to an orderly who saw Tom out of the office. 'When I heard about your loss,' the Captain begin,' I just couldn't believe it. As God is my judge, it was a full week before I learned of the railroad's men who had been killed that day also. I know it's early, but have you given any thought to what you'll be doing now that it's just you and the boy?'

'Not really,' Simon said. 'Then again, I can tell you honestly that I can't count how many thoughts have passed through my mind considering just what I'll do. I'm leaning to staying right here so as to be near Darlene.

'Then again I've a business venture purchasing lumber for settlers that is doing well. Paul Atkins is in this effort with me. And now with the added settlers setting down roots, the gun sales have increased considerably. But as I said, I really don't know what tomorrow brings for me.

'I will say that if I decide to go back east, you'll be the first to know after my neighbor Tom. However, I've been thinking about my son. He'll be needing an education as he grows older, and I don't see that as possibly out here, least wise not a book learning education. I'm believing a proper school somewhere back east for the boy is the answer.

'Now, I hate like Hell to have to say this to you, but I never learned my letters. My Darlene always covered that failing for me. I'd be appreciative if you'd consider writing a letter for me and sending it to Richard Jarvis at Colt. He is my son's Godfather and I see him as a way for the boy getting an education while at the same time it would be buying time for me. Eventually, I could go back east, or once the boy is finished school, he could come back out and join me here. Now I'll be asking you, as a friend, what do you think of this idea?'

'I'd be honored to write a letter for you. I also have contacts in the east that I can lean on. Those contacts have kept me here when I was sure I'd be replaced after the Indian hanging incident. An education would give the boy a big leg up whether he stays in the east or returns out here. I'll have a couple of letters ready for the next stage or train going east. Soon as I hear anything from my letters, or an answer from Mister Jarvis I'll notify you.'

Later outside, Simon saw Tom standing by the wagon. Young Simon was talking with some children his age over by where the Indians had been camped. Approaching Tom, he asked what he thought of Fort Kearney.

'Well,' Tom said, 'it's grown some since I was last here. And the price of hides is more than I ever thought I'd be getting. Now those hides were nothing to me, they were just taking up space in my cabin. So with the money I got for them, I figure I'll be buying a pistol off you provided you'll sell it to me at full value. I won't be accepting anything less.

'As for the rest of the money I've no use for it. I figure I'll give it to you to hold for your son. Now down the line, I'll be paying more attention to the animals I shoot, and taking pains when I work their hides. I've always believed in a good steak, and now I'll be thinking on the money I can get for the coat the animal was wearing also.'

A week later back at the homestead, Simon was in deep thought as to just what he'd be doing now that his world had taken such an abrupt change. He'd given a lot of thought to having his son get a proper education and felt comfortable with the thought of that schooling happening in the east. For the present he was also comfortable with staying at his homestead here in Lexington. The lumber and gun sales were going well, and he was putting aside money that he suspected would cover the cost of an eastern education for his son. Once a week he'd ride up to where Darlene was buried and spend the better part of a day at her grave. On those days his son would be off fishing, or visiting with Tom.

It was now October 1876 and the first snow was settling down upon the higher mountains and hills of Nebraska. Simon found it hard to believe all that had transpired in his life. He remembered his days as a slave on the plantation in South Carolina as though it were only yesterday. Then while thinking about being in Providence Rhode Island and his journey west, he found it difficult to realize the war had been over for eleven years now, and his son was now eight years old.

Six weeks later Simon received word from Richard Jarvis. 'Not only will young Simon get a first class education, but I'll insure that he'll experience a home life here in

Connecticut also. When not in school, I will introduce him to my family and friends along with the firearms business here at Colt.' That evening Simon spoke with his son regarding the news from Richard Jarvis.

'I'd like to stay right here,' young Simon said. 'I guess it would be good to be able to write, but I don't really see my having a need for any school learning. While living at the fort I learned enough to know how to sign my name so people can read it. I figure I can learn a little more staying right here as time goes by. You and Tom are here, I can't see as my going east would make any sense.'

'I never had any book learning myself,' Simon said to his son. 'But I've been to a number of places that when I was a little older I hadn't known existed. Since then I've come to see that the more a body knows, the better off he is. Now I'll tell you true, it wasn't easy for me to tell the Captain at the fort that I couldn't write any, and to ask him to write a letter for me. But it was just something I really believed I had to do, not for me but for you.

'Now slavery is a thing of the past, but I'm thinking the bad things of slavery will always be with us. Them that have an education will always be on top of us that don't. I'm set in my ways, but you are young enough to learn and grow yourself up to a level in life far better than I'll ever know. Your Mother and I both wanted this for you.

'And this world is changing quicker than we ever

imagined. Today we've the railroad and trains that connect us out here with places back east like Hartford in Connecticut. What took your mother and me months to cross over land to get here, today wagons coming west are just about ending. Now people can come here from just about anywhere back east, and be setting down new roots in just a few weeks.

'When you are back east the time will pass quicker than you can imagine. I promise you that we won't be apart very long. And before you know it, I'll be asking you to write a letter for me instead of my feeling low and having to ask Captain Turner.'

Three weeks later, young Simon Washington Jackson was on a train going east. Simon and Tom saw him off at the station, knowing Richard Jarvis would be waiting at Hartford for the boy's arrival. Paul Atkins had seen to it that a member of the railroad would accompany the boy throughout the complete journey.

The following day Simon spent several hours at Darlene's grave. 'Our boy is going east to get an education,' he said while kneeling beside the marker he'd set when he'd buried Darlene. 'I know deep down this has been the right thing to do, but it's only been a few hours now and already it's tearing me apart inside. I dread waking up tomorrow and our boy not being here. Right this minute, I swear if I thought I could catch that train taking him away, I'd be on a horse chasing it down.

'Old Tom has been a God send! He sold some fur when we went to the fort to tell Captain Mark Turner what happened when the Cheyenne attacked our place. Then he gave me all the money he got for the pelts. Part of it was for a pistol he bought from me, but the bulk of the money was for me to put aside for our son. Beyond that, Tom's been staying by me like a mother hen. Every day he cooks up something and sets it in front of me to eat. He's also brought over a mess of traps and started showing me the proper way to set them. If nothing more, it's something to take my mind off you and the boy not being with me.'

Beginning the first week of November 1876, half a foot of fresh snow blanketed Lexington. With this true start of winter, Tom and Simon began setting out traps a good mile north of the homestead.

Four new families had staked out plots of land to homestead beside the Platte River a mile and a half west of Simon's location. They said they would winter at the fort, and paid Simon for lumber to be delivered at their site come spring. Simon handed the money to Captain Mark Turner asking him to forward it to Richard Jarvis at Colt in payment for pistols sold, and to request another shipment. Stopping at the railroad Depot, he wired Paul requesting he arrange for the next shipment of lumber. He also inquired of Paul regarding the possibility of getting a safe, or having one at the Depot made available to him. Having the depot manager verify the money collected for lumber, this money was set in the safe in a leather pouch Paul had earlier provided.

Chapter 11
Time Moves On

"Throughout the first winter without Darleen and young Simon, Tom and I worked a trap line we had established. Trapping both sides of the Platte, the line we established required a full day to traverse. Thankfully, the Indian situation remained calm throughout the winter. On March first 1877, I caught my first beaver in a trap I'd set all by myself. Tom heard me hollering and ran toward the sound. Coming into view, he saw me dancing around the beaver I had pulled from the water and had it now lying at my feet."

'Well, I swear you must have been really listening to me when I explained how to set a trap for beaver,' Tom said as he slapped Simon on the back. 'Still got all your fingers?' Tom asked as he grabbed Simon's hands and pulled them toward him. Kneeling and rubbing his hand across the dead beaver Tom said, 'That's a prime hide if ever I saw one, and I'll admit to seeing quite a few in my younger trapping days. When we get home I'll show you how to scrape and clean this critter so as to get a decent amount of money for the hide. Trapping is just about a dead business now-a-days. But there is still a dollar or two to be made off a good pelt like this.'

"By early May, every sign of snow and ice was gone from the valley. New grasses had pushed up four inches out of the soil. In April, I had planted most of what would be in my garden area. But standing in the garden, I always believed I saw Darlene standing several feet away as I'd seen her on that last day when she had died. Now at age thirty-four, for the very first time in my life I felt lost. Darlene was gone, never again to share her wickedness or her passion with me. My son was in Connecticut getting the education both Darlene and I had wanted young Simon to have. There was an emptiness that now bore down on me with a weight such as I had never known.

"Recently signs of days-gone-by and segregation's past was rearing its ugly head once again brought on by some southerners who'd come west. They were not pleased to see a black man so prominent in this area that they now chose to settle in. I had helped many people settling in Lexington. I was the one that could make finished lumber available to the new settlers. I was also the sole area representative of Colt Firearms. With the hostile Indian situation still uppermost in people's minds, protection and a sense of safety were available at my front door. No one person in particular stood out or came forward, but the suspicion that racial trouble was brewing began to be felt throughout the settlement. Two men up from Alabama had built a saw-mill a mile northwest of the train depot. Within one year, they were producing enough rough saw-cut lumber to meet the needs of new arrivals. With Fort Kearney now abandoned by the military, the town named Kearney developed where the settlement of Dobytown had existed earlier.

"I was aware of the changes taking place around me. Tom had died during the Christmas Season of 1877, leaving another large void in my life. Contacting Paul Atkins, I advised Paul of the new lumber mill north of the Depot and suggested we cease suppling lumber by Union Pacific Rail to Lexington. Writing to Richard Jarvis at Colt Firearms, I reported that my inventory included twenty-five Colt pistols and five rifles. I stated that I intended selling these while looking for someone to replace me as a representative of Colt Firearms.

"In January of 1878, I placed my claim on fifty acres of land located where I'd buried Darlene. Within one week a couple from Virginia bought my original homestead in Lexington. When I was satisfied that the winter snows were behind me, I began clearing a section of land where I would build my new home.

"One hundred yards south of Darlene's gravesite, I staked out the corner locations for my house. On a slope of land behind where my home would be, I also set cornerstones for a fifty-foot barn. Now for the first time in several months I didn't feel alone or without purpose. I had fulfilled Darleen's request that if I moved from the homestead, I would relocate to this site that so pleased her with the natural blooms of goldenrod and wildflowers. Once again, I had found purpose in my life.

"When Paul Atkins learned of my new adventure, he sent three men, employed by the Union Pacific as carpenters, to assist me with building my new homestead and barn. At the same time, he advised me that he was putting in a claim for fifty acres and that he intended homesteading once he retired from the Union Pacific. The acreage he was claiming butted up against my land. As the summer of 1878 drew to a close, I was satisfied with the progress we'd made at my new homestead. I was thankful for the assistance Paul had provided with having three accomplished-carpenters helping me in getting my house built. During the building it seemed that windows, doors, and beautiful finished wood often arrived at the train depot, supplied by my generous friend."

'Don't give it a second thought,' one of the carpenters said to Simon while chuckling. 'Paul is also taking care of himself, you can lay money on that. From what I've seen already, there is enough building material laid aside at Kearney, just waiting for Paul to arrive and start working on his own homestead. And I don't doubt but that Bill, Ernest and I will be right back here working along beside him.

'Paul has taken care of us for many a year while building and laying track for the Union Pacific. Paul has done right by us and by the Union Pacific, and that's the truth. He doesn't have to look over his shoulder one little bit. The higher-ups at the railroad know they've gotten one hundred percent from Paul from the day when he began working for them.'

"As July 4ᵗʰ, 1878 approached, my new home was complete. Bill, Ernest and John had packed up and left in order to return to the Union Pacific site where Paul was still working. My house had been completely closed in by mid-June. Now on this one hundredth-third birthday/ anniversary of the country, I thought back over everything that had passed in my life. I was an American! Africa was a time in my life I no longer thought or cared about. The plantation at Pemberton had become a distant memory.

"I thought peacefully about my friend Blue, along with Martha and several other slaves I'd known while at Pemberton. I thought about Darlene's first husband, Jonathan, and the overseer James Temper. Today I remembered Blue working at changing his speech so as to remove all trace of his African heritage. I chuckled to myself when I remembered how Captain Mark Turner had voiced his thought that I was a free black originally from Connecticut. 'I detect a strong nutmeg Yankee tone in your voice,' Mark had said when he first talked with me.

"Yes, so much had passed in my life. Now I was in Nebraska, Indian Territory, where my wife, the love of my life, had been killed by raiding Cheyenne Indians and laid to rest not a hundred yards from where I was now standing.

"Our only child, young Simon, was off in Connecticut enrolled in an academy getting a proper education. Next year young Simon would be finished with his initial schooling and be returning to Lexington. I looked at the house and large barn, then slowly turned taking into view the mountains off to the northwest. Lowering my gaze, I looked at the low wrought-iron work that surrounded Darlene's resting place. I wondered what my son would think of all this after being in such a big city back east.

"We'll do just fine," Simon whispered to himself.

"Having been asked by Richard Jarvis of Colt firearms to continue on as the representative of Colt, I bought a small building in Lexington and opened it as a Colt Firearms outpost store. A minimal amount of stock was kept at this store, while the bulk of my inventory was kept secure in my barn at home. Having stopped the shipment of finished lumber arriving at Lexington appeared to erase the tension that had developed with the men at the new sawmill. In six months' time, I began to feel comfortable with my new station in life and my surroundings. The Army had engaged and defeated several small bands of young warriors, pushing most of the Indians out of Nebraska.

"A new era had arrived. With the establishment of the railroad, new towns were springing up across the state. Now bank and train robbers were appearing on the front page of newspapers, replacing Indian concerns. Communities were growing, and a new attitude among the people was developing. In the fall planning was begun regarding building a bandstand near the center of Lexington with the intent of having this project completed in time for the one hundredth-fifth anniversary of the country, and the eleventh anniversary of Nebraska Statehood. With all the building that was taking place, a volunteer fire brigade had been formed and the latest fire equipment available was ordered at Omaha. In early September 1878, I was approached and asked to sit on the town's planning committee.

"On June twelfth of 1879, I was standing on the railroad

depot platform when engine number 0-8 slowly pulled to a stop. Young Simon stepped out of the second carriage and ran toward me. Strapped to his hip was a presentation-model Colt, highly engraved and resting in a buff-colored holster.

'I've brought you some books from the academy,' his son said after they were seated in the carriage Simon had brought to the depot. 'In no time at all, together, I'll have you reading and writing. Gosh, but it's good to be home.'

Simon looked at his son who was now going on eleven years of age and smiled. 'Now I just might put my whole heart and soul into some book-learning seeing as I'm now a member of the town's planning committee,' Simon said. 'But we've some time to catch up on you and me so we'll just take it one day at a time. I want to hear all about your time in Hartford, and God knows there has been a lot that's happened around here since you went off back east.' Before leaving town, Simon took his son past the house they'd built and lived in after first arriving in Lexington. Then he stopped in front of the small gun store a block west of where the bandstand was to be built. It was just after noon when Simon turned the carriage onto the drive leading to their new home. Stopping short of the house, Simon pointed over at Darlene's gravesite. Without speaking, his son left the wagon and walked over to the grave.

Young Simon was pleased with all that his father had done regarding this site. Looking up at the mountains, then back down over at the house and barn, he believed his mother was resting peaceably at this location. Walking back to his father, he caught up with him just as Simon was standing, waiting to enter the house.

Unbuckling the gun belt and holster he handed the weapon to his father. 'This is actually a present to you from Richard Jarvis,' he said. 'I've only worn it since it made me feel closer to you as I was coming back here from out east. Richard gave me a somewhat plainer pistol and holster that I treasure and have kept in my suitcase. Your Colt pistol was engraved by Gustave Young. I believe he is the best of the best, and I actually watched him doing the engraving on this cylinder.'

"So there you have my story," Simon said. "I'm sorry I rambled on like I did, but while telling you all this, the memories just came flooding back. Now I have my son back with me and my life is complete. I don't have a clue as to what tomorrow will bring for me and the boy, but now if your editor choses to print this tale, at least the questions about me that you say are out there, I hope will have been answered."

Jessie pushed back her chair, stood up, and shook Simon's outstretched hand. "I truly believe it is a shame that I only have sketchy notes of all you have told me. I look forward to meeting your son, and would have given anything to have met Darleen. As to your future, I have to believe the people of Lexington are far from hearing the last from you. I hope you will stop in and visit when you are in the area. We both know where there is some excellent whiskey to toast to our friendship!"

"Well, Miss Jessie, I'll be sure to bring my son around so you can meet him. He is a fine young man, but I'm sure any father would say the same about his own flesh and blood. And I won't forget your invite to share a small glass with you. I'll be sure to stop by when your article is printed!"

Simon chuckled as he stepped outside. Taking a few minutes to think about all he had said within that office these past few days, he smiled as he realized that a weight had been lifted off him. Today was a new day, and the past he'd experienced finally presented him with a new clean slate.

As the year 1885 arrived, Simon was elected Mayor of Lexington. He and his son had started a school that served Indian, Black, and White children alike. As fresh snow fell on the bustling town of Lexington, eighteen children entered a schoolhouse for the first time in their lives.

"The past belongs in a history book," Simon said to his son. "It's time now people here-a-bout set their thoughts on this new century we're coming up to. Why, just think what we can accomplish if we all set our minds to it!"

On the day that the town's new bandstand was dedicated, Simon signed his name to the proclamation that would be entered into the town's records. Pausing, he looked at his signature on the paper, smiled, and then while wiping tears from his eyes, whispered to himself, "Who'd a thought?"

Before Simon died, many changes had come to Lexington. The town's dirt streets had been paved. Wagons gave way to automobiles. Miss Jessie became the editor of the Lexington

News and young Simon had married a doctor named Alice, who had come out from the east wanting to see the frontier, much as his own mother did, before it ceased to be. Finally, all had come full circle!

Afterword

I truly enjoyed writing this novel. My earlier books: *Abenaki Autumn,_Pathway to Liberty*, and *Goodbye For A While*, also brought me a certain amount of pleasure, as many kind people have expressed enjoyment in reading my stories while asking when my next novel would be available.

There are few feelings comparable to that of seeing your first novel in print. There is an excitement to a new book as you first take it from the box the publisher has sent to you. For well over a year or often longer, you have labored writing and rewriting different chapters, changing and embellishing characters that you've seen vividly in your mind. Now for the very first time, the colors of your novel leap at you from the cover. And there is also a special publishers printing smell about a new book that cannot be denied. Twelve years have passed since my first novel went into print. Yet even today I manage to keep a copy of that first book beside my computer.

My first novel, *Abenaki Autumn* won a Writer's Digest International Book Award, which only elevated my pleasure of having completed a task I'd set as a goal when I'd first sat down intending to write a positive novel about Native Americans. Writing that first novel also opened a totally new world I had not ever given thought to. My book signings, either locally or at various historical locations occurred from Florida to Canada. I had a group of six Abenaki Natives arrive at one book signing. They expressed their pleasure at finally reading a book that spoke to their culture in a most positive way.

With *Pathway To Liberty*, reality was beginning to set in. Local stores and gift shops at historical sites insist on forty present profit if they were to display and sell your novel. As a self-published writer, ten present profit was the norm. So, it came down to person to person sales, along with sales at Amazon and Barnes and Noble. Yet still, there were encouragements never anticipated resulting in book sales.

Recently, a lady came upon one of my novels while visiting a nursing home. She enjoyed the reading so much that she tracked me down as the author, and bought my other two novels. A man I golfed with enjoyed my novels to the extent that he ordered several more copies that he gave as gifts to friends. On a cruise ship, a friend pointed out a lady to me that was relaxing by the pool, reading one of my novels. Approaching her, I lifted the book from her while turning to the back cover that held my picture and pointed at the back cover and myself. To say she was excited would be an understatement. Yes, I signed her copy.

Goodbye For A While was a pleasure to write. It also expanded on research that needed to be done. Many visits to Charleston and Savannah, along with in-depth tours of several Civil War era plantations, brought a true realism to its pages. One could not honestly write about the Boone Plantation, without having gone there and walked those historic grounds. The many thousands of hand-made bricks from these plantations, can be seen today in Charleston, along with Fort Sumter.

Their Chosen Home was once again a chance to bring characters from a previous work forward into a new setting. It was also a chance to show how people can change. Someone portrayed earlier as evil such as Darlene, could do a complete turn around and become a very special person, while the worth of another individual could be elevated from slavery to freedom.

In this story's telling, I hoped to also define the changes in America that were taking place as wagon-trains and people went west. Leaving behind them was the era of whale oil and sailing ships, Iron Men and Wooden Ships as it was often described in our country at the time. Young children working in factories throughout the east would also become a thing of the past. The opening, along with the settling of our west was observed around the world, and a new expanded vocabulary came into being, cattlemen and sodbusters, barbed wire and gunslingers just to name a few of the words that became purely American fixtures in our language. New icons stepped forward onto America's stage with the opening of the west: Buffalo Bill, Kit Carson, Sitting Bull and Crazy Horse, Calamity Jane, John Freemont and Davy Crockett to name just a few. Places they set foot upon would in time become our National Parks.

This latest novel, *Their Chosen Home*, focused on westward expansion. While doing research for my book, the following entry was most helpful:

NE History & Record of Pioneer Days, Vol. VII, no.2 (part 1) pages 33 – 35 contained an article about a committee chosen to award a prize of $100 for a poem suitable for the semi-centennial anniversary of Nebraska in 1917. Several hundred poems were received by the committee and the odes were graded on meter, spontaneity, dignity, appeal, individuality of thought, harmony, and poetic beauty. The winning poem, *HYMN TO NEBRASKA*, was submitted by Rev. William H. Buss of Fremont, Nebraska in 1916. Mr. Buss was pastor of the Congregational Church of Fremont. We chose the third stanza as it truly represented this novel as it could well have been titled, *Simon's Tale:*

III

The foothills of the Rockies lie
Afar athwart her western sky;
Her rolling prairie, like the sea,
Held long in virgin sanctity,
Her fertile loam.

Her wild-life roamed o'er treeless plains,
Till came the toiling wagon-trains,
And settlers bold, far westward bound,
In broad Nebraska's valleys found,
THEIR CHOSEN HOME.

CPSIA information can be obtained
at www.ICGtesting.com
Printed in the USA
BVHW041923271120
594367BV00034B/689